WITCH WITH A BADGE

WITCH WITH A BADGE

WITCH WARRIOR™ BOOK 1

TR CAMERON MARTHA CARR MICHAEL ANDERLE

This book is a work of fiction. All of the characters, organizations, and events portrayed in this novel are either products of the author's imagination or are used fictitiously. Sometimes both.

A Michael Anderle Production

LMBPN Publishing
PMB 196, 2540 South Maryland Pkwy
Las Vegas, NV 89109

Version 1.00, May 2022
ebook ISBN: 979-8-88541-195-0
Print ISBN: 979-8-88541-623-8

DEDICATION

Dedication: For those who seek wonder around every corner and in each turning page. Thank you choosing to share the adventure with me. And, as always, for Dylan and Laurel, my reasons for existing.

— TR Cameron

THE WITCH WITH A BADGE TEAM

Thanks to our beta readers:
Larry Omans, John Ashmore, Angela Wood, Kelly O'Donnell

Thanks to our JIT Readers:

Zacc Pelter
Diane L. Smith
Peter Manis
Dorothy Lloyd
Dave Hicks

If we've missed anyone, please let us know!

Editor
SkyFyre Editing Team

CHAPTER ONE

Compared to Cait's previous experience at the US Marshals' office in Columbus, Ohio, the scene as she entered Boston's John Joseph Moakley Federal Courthouse on Monday morning was one of barely controlled chaos. People moved in all directions through the lobby after passing through the metal, magic, and explosive detectors at the door and having their bags searched. She'd shown her ID and temporarily surrendered the cardboard box of personal and professional items she carried in both arms for inspection on the way in.

In one corner, a guide addressed a group of tourists, detailing the building's notable architectural features. It was an environment that tempered utility with beauty, from the interior artworks to the sweeping glass-front curved exterior. Cait shook her head. *Not the most secure location on the planet, that's for sure, but the guards and inspectors look competent, and the place has managed for quite a long time before Caitriona Eloise Keane ever set foot inside. It prob-*

ably isn't about to succumb to some random unpleasantness on my first visit, I hope.

Cait stepped into the elevator with a dozen others, riding up to the top level. Those around her wore suits or dresses, everyone on their best behavior for a day in court as defendant, lawyer, jury, or maybe judge. She wore the same outfit she'd worn to her first day on the job in Columbus, a black business suit over a deep red blouse and stylish boots that climbed to her calves underneath her pants. Her right wrist bore her only jewelry other than the small silver studs in her earlobes, a bracelet of twined metal and wood with a turquoise stone set into it. People often noticed it, and she accepted their compliments with the explanation that it was a family heirloom.

That was accurate as far as it went but was also a lie by omission. The wooden parts had indeed belonged to her great-grandmother. Cait had used her power to reshape her ancestor's wand into something she could wear around her wrist. It allowed her to bring the magic that was her heritage as a witch into play without digging for a casting implement. *Which is handy in my rather active line of work.*

The doors opened on the top level, and she strode out, making a left to head to her new office. She'd liked Columbus and would have been happy to stay, but when the opportunity to jump to the much bigger city had appeared, she'd accepted it without hesitation. *And without much transition time since my last day there was Friday.* She stepped through the outer glass door with a professional smile and was surprised to see several people striding toward her. *That's quite the welcome wagon for a new employee.* One of them, an older man in a trim business suit with an unruly bundle of white hair said, "Keane. Welcome in."

She nodded guardedly. "Thanks, Chief Levitt."

His lined face rearranged itself as he smiled. "Call me Simon." He gestured in turn at the two men next to him. "This is Clement Austin, and this is Garrett Bradley." The former was tan and healthy-looking, held himself ramrod straight, and seemed simultaneously muscular and lanky. He had collar-length blond hair with the sides slicked back.

The latter was bald, with dark black skin reflecting the lights above. His body strained a little at his suit, like he'd let himself go a little. His brilliant smile lit up the room. Levitt's head tipped toward the corner of the room. "Over there is Sabrina Morin." The woman he indicated seemed reserved, and the most notable thing about her was the darkness of her hair against the paleness of her skin. "Everyone, this is our new deputy marshal, Cait Keane." He turned back to her. "Good. Introductions are over. Grab your gear. We've got a situation."

Twenty minutes later, Cait was in the rear seat of a dark SUV with tinted windows, sealing the last Velcro strap on her bulletproof vest. *Good thing I wore a long-sleeve blouse.* Her suit jacket was too well-tailored to go over the body armor, and showing off her abundant tattoos on day one probably wouldn't be a great choice, even though the USMS didn't prohibit them.

Garrett was behind the wheel, and Clement rode shotgun. She presumed Chief Levitt was in his own vehicle, but she'd lost track of him as they hustled toward the garage beside the courthouse. A quick check confirmed that her pistol was properly seated in her shoulder holster, and her vest hadn't dislodged it. *Dressing in the car is an art form I haven't had to practice for a while. Welcome to Boston, Cait.*

Clement turned to face her and nodded. "Good. You're ready. Add these to your loadout." That phrasing plus a couple of other things he'd said, and his general demeanor, told her that he was ex-military. She'd trained with people like him at Glynco and served with several as part of her work with the Marshals' Special Operations Group. She accepted the two small boxes and clipped the first onto her belt behind her hip, pulling on it to ensure it was secure. It was a communication base station, a model she was well familiar with.

The other box held a pair of large glasses with temples that hooked over the ears, and she slipped them on. The lenses darkened slightly in response to the sunlight coming through the windshield, and data appeared around the periphery of her visual field as the eyewear went through its diagnostic process. She said, "Radio check," when prompted by the glasses.

A woman's voice replied, "I can hear you."

Clement asked, "Morin, what do we know?"

Sabrina, who was apparently their coordinator with the home office while they were in the field, answered, "I've got him on traffic cameras. Drone inbound, ETA seventy seconds. He's gone into an old apartment building. Six floors, four units on each floor. Target has no obvious connection to anyone inside."

Those were the first real operational details Cait had

received and restraining herself from seeking them had been getting increasingly difficult. Before she could ask for clarification, Clement said, "Our target is Mitchell Walsman. He's a federal fugitive who woke up, decided today would be a great day to do something stupid, and stopped by to visit a former girlfriend."

She replied, "True love?"

Sabrina laughed, a throaty sound with a sarcastic edge. "Hardly. He tried to break into her apartment while screaming loud enough for the entire neighborhood to hear that he was going to kill her. Fortunately, she installed a heavy door after he went inside when she cut ties. We've kept an eye on her place, along with the known associates of any federal fugitive with connections to Boston. The computers gave us the heads-up when he showed."

Cait replied, "Impressive."

Chief Levitt's voice joined the conversation. "One of the great things about being in a big town is that we have the money for nice toys and local brainpower to help create them." From behind the wheel, Garrett lifted his hand, opening and closing his fingertips to mimic flapping gums. She grinned as Levitt finished, "Austin has tactical command. Morin is your liaison. I'll be listening in and coordinating with local PD."

Clement said dryly, "Best if the boys in blue don't get in the way."

The chief barked a laugh. "I'm aware of your opinion on the local constabulary, Austin. They'll maintain their distance until they're needed. So, try not to make them needed."

"Roger that." Clement's voice held a touch of a southern

accent, and she imagined he could probably turn the good old boy charm on and off at will. "We'll rely on the drone to take care of the roof and go in together on the ground floor."

He opened the glove compartment and extended a pistol magazine to her. "Our target is part elf or something. You might need this." She accepted it and looked inside, finding the telltale blue glow of anti-magic ammunition at the tip of the rounds.

Cait wasn't sure whether the chief had shared the knowledge that she was a magical with the rest of the team. In her previous job, her boss had preferred she keep it quiet for reasons he'd never chosen to explain. *Which is one of the things that pushed me out of Columbus. Like my mother is fond of saying, I've gotta be me.* She inwardly laughed as she slipped the magazine into a loop on her vest.

With no hint of warning, Garrett yelled, "*Bail! Bail! Bail!*" Her body reacted before her mind fully processed the words. She slammed open the door to her left, hit the release on her seatbelt, and hurled herself out of the rapidly decelerating vehicle as she exerted her magic to cover herself in a force shield.

She hit the pavement a moment before a fireball slammed into the SUV, flipping it onto its hood and sending it skidding forward several feet. Sparks flew as it scraped along the road. She saw the initial impact in flashes as she tumbled but had stopped moving as it landed, ablaze from the magical attack.

Clement snapped, "Check in."

She half-growled, half-groaned, "Keane, undamaged."

Garrett confirmed his well-being with a snarled, "Bradley, seriously pissed off."

Clement was already running toward the building, and she moved into a jog to follow him to the cover it offered. "I'd say he knows we're here."

He laughed. "Yeah. Just once, I'd like to reach a place by stealth."

Garrett countered sarcastically, "That's for the weasels in the Paranormal Defense Agency and government Special Ops. We're the Marshals. Our targets should quake in fear."

Clement replied, "Okay. Focus up. Here we go."

CHAPTER TWO

Cait moved up beside Clement near the double entrance doors of the apartment building. Garrett arrived on the opposite side, shaking his head. "The rifles were in the car."

Clement replied, "Couldn't have used them. Too many innocents."

"And the shotguns."

"Okay, that's a loss." Cait drew her pistol and ensured it was ready for action. Clement continued, "I'll lead. Keane, middle. Bradley, watch our backs." She frowned inwardly but kept her professional face frozen. *Don't trust me yet. Totally understandable, but I'd forgotten how much being the new kid on the block sucks.*

She tapped her glasses to disable her mic and whispered, "Earth around me, hear my plea, eyes and ears of the owl, I request of thee," completing the invocation with a small gesture of her right arm. The tingle of active magic flowed through her body, the rightness of it always a pleasurable sensation.

Neither of her partners appeared to have noticed her action, which was good since the status of magicals at her new job was still in question. *Gonna have to push the chief on that.* She'd gotten very skilled at casting surreptitious spells in her last city. If she had to continue to do it in Boston, despite how suboptimal that would be, she was prepared to do so.

Clement grabbed the handle and pushed the door in. She followed him into the lobby, moving to the right as he continued forward. As the doors closed behind Garret a moment after, Clement ordered, "Tell PD to seal off the street."

Morin replied with a curt, "Acknowledged."

The building's entry area was old-looking, with tarnished metal mailboxes set in one wall, cracked linoleum on the floor, and dim lighting struggling to escape from dirty fixtures on the walls. A staircase marched around the building's inner perimeter, giving access to the four apartments at each level. An open shaft ran up the center, and she leaned forward for a moment's look at the skylight at its crown before jerking her head out of the potential line of fire.

Elevator doors of grimy silver metal, one of them dented, stood at one side of a column that extended through the tall shaft. Clement nodded at it. "Keane, want to take the easy way up?"

His tone was joking, but Cait recognized it for the test it was. *A stupid one.* "One fireball, it's a convection oven. Two, and it's a free-falling crematorium. I'm good. Didn't have time to do my cardio before work, anyway."

He laughed. "Onward and upward."

As they reached the first floor with guns drawn, keeping them pointed at the doorways as they moved across the landing, a harsh voice called down from above. "Hey. Assholes."

Garrett said, "I think he's talking to you, Austin."

Clement shouted, "Name-calling isn't nice. How about you come down here with your hands raised, and we do this without any undue pain and suffering?"

The chatter of an automatic rifle accompanied the sound of bullets whizzing by in the staircase's central open area. Cait commented, "I think that's a no. I may be wrong here, but my instincts tell me he's not very nice. Wonder if he's alone up there." *If so, one lightning blast could end this problem.*

Unfortunately, Clement confirmed what her display glasses were showing her. "Too many thermal signatures to be confident of that. Morin?"

Sabrina replied, "Drone doesn't give any clear sense of who's who, but shows a lot of people inside the apartments on every level."

Garrett asked, "Isn't that supposed to be what your fancy drones are good for?"

"Bite me."

The comment drew a laugh from Cait. "I'm going to fit in perfectly with you folks. Do you have any useful information on the building's residents?"

Sabrina answered, "Other than the most basic stuff, like names, employment, and demographics, none."

Garrett said, "Thanks for the help as always, Morin."

Sabrina's sarcasm was evident. "For you, sweetie? Anytime."

Clement interrupted, "All right. Push forward. We don't shoot unarmed people, but if someone's holding a weapon, they go down."

Cait followed his footsteps precisely, four feet behind, her enhanced senses picking out conversations while she watched the space ahead of them for potential traps. The former provided no information she could use, and the latter revealed nothing dangerous awaiting them. *Except for the chucklehead still firing blindly down the stairwell.* She said, "Apparently, he's got a lot of ammunition."

Garrett confirmed, "Seems like."

The gunfire stopped as they reached the fifth floor, and they heard a door bang closed on the level above. Clement shook his head. "I guess it was too much to ask that he'd stay out there being a good target."

She replied, "Guess so."

"I don't like it." He paused for a moment, then continued, "Here's what we're going to do. We rush up and get to the far wall on either side of the farthest apartment's door. Keane and I cover one through three, and Bradley watches the fourth, ready to yell loud and proud if any danger comes from that angle."

The other man replied, "Affirmative." She echoed the response.

"Okay. Here we go." Clement raced forward up the remaining steps, heading for the defensive position he'd chosen. When they reached the top level, all four doors opened and discharged enemies. They weren't carrying guns, which was good news, but they didn't reveal the other weapons they held until they were too close for gunfire, which was less positive.

Cait rammed her pistol into her shoulder holster and engaged the nearest new arrival. The man was easily half again her size, his stature a mixture of muscle and fat, with uneven stubble on his head. He whipped a metal pipe around at her skull with a look of eager anticipation while grabbing her arm with his other hand. She circled her right arm from inside to out, blocking his grip before it could stabilize, and lifted her left arm to keep the pipe from coming in from behind as she stepped in close.

She slammed a knee up, but he twisted to catch the blow on his thigh. At this near distance, his size was a disadvantage as she'd intended. While he tried to draw his long arms back to attack her, she released her block, clenched her fists, and delivered simultaneous straight punches to his groin and sternum. He made a choking noise and hit the floor. She stepped on him and launched herself at the next in a jump kick.

This opponent was closer to her size, so Cait had no trouble landing the leaping roundhouse to the side of his head. He raised an arm to block, but her momentum overwhelmed the hasty defense. He slammed sideways to bounce off the wall, then slumped to the floor.

She landed in perfect balance, looking for her next target. At that moment, a blast of magic flew out of one of the apartments, smashing into Garrett. Fortunately, it was force rather than fire. More fortunately, the attacker hadn't had sufficient ability to strike hard enough to make the blow instantly fatal.

Unfortunately, it knocked him stumbling backward. The backs of his legs hit the too-low-for-code banister, and he flipped over it, the remaining force of the blast propelling him too far away to grab at the railing as he found himself with only six stories of empty air beneath him.

Cait yelled, "Austin, be right back," as she dove over the banister, launching herself after Garrett.

CHAPTER THREE

Time seemed to pass in slow motion as Cait plummeted a story above Garrett. His face was turned up toward her, his expression one of complete shock, and she wondered if he was seeing his life play out before his eyes as all the stories said. She, facing down, had a perfect perspective of how fast the floor was coming up beneath them. *Better get this done quick.*

She released the enhanced senses spell she'd been holding, thrust her right arm forward, and willed her force magic into readiness. She traced lines from side to side, building out the spell as she wanted it to be, then discharged the gathered power. A burst of magic shot down, and one story above the floor snapped magical ropes out to every surface, creating a landing web.

He hit a moment before she did and sank into the yielding magic that stretched almost to the linoleum before bouncing him gently back up. She struck hard, her less central position and the fact that the web was coming upward to meet her making the end of her descent a bruising one. Her breath exploded out of her, and she lay there for a moment, focusing on regaining it. Beside her, Garrett breathed, "Holy shit. I was sure I was dead. How am I not dead?"

Cait rolled over, pushed herself up to her hands and knees, and climbed to her feet on the unsteady surface. "Your lucky day, I guess. Sorry about this." His look of confusion inspired an inner smile. Then she blasted force magic in a column down to the ground, causing the web to twist and toss him to the side. She lacked the control to truly fly but was adept at hurling herself through the air. Her path bent in a shallow arc toward her top floor destination.

She realized about three-quarters of the way up that she wouldn't make it. With a quiet growl, Cait snapped out a band of force magic that snagged the edge of the skylight, allowing her to use her momentum to swing over to the sixth-floor platform.

She landed on the banister, rocked for a moment before catching her balance, and leapt for the nearest enemy. Clement was backed into a corner, defending himself against blows from a trio of people. He'd managed to liberate a pipe from someone and was using it to block stabs from a switchblade, to counter occasional swings from a baseball bat, and to force the third assailant back when he tried to engage. The threesome would've been more effective as a duo, which would have given them room to work without interfering with one another's efforts. *Thank heaven for stupid criminals.*

Cait crashed into an unengaged foe. Her knees slammed into his shoulder as he turned too late to face the threat and knocked him to the ground with the sound of breaking bone. When her boots touched the floor, she dropped and spun into a leg sweep, knocking the next closest off his feet. She didn't take the time to finish him but sprang at another who had reacted quickly enough to swing an oversized carpenter's hammer at her in a wicked arc.

She coated her right arm in force magic and blocked the strike, enjoying his look of surprise a moment before her front kick crashed into his sternum, stealing his breath and sending him flying. He slammed into one of the three besieging Clement, and her fellow marshal used the distraction to escape the corner, heading toward her.

The other two who had been attacking him turned. She resisted the urge to draw her pistol and shoot them, not knowing for sure what was behind them and imagining that the walls of this old building were probably thin, brittle, or both. She dashed at the one on her left, who brandished his switchblade at her, and Clement took the one on the right. Moments later, both were down, hers with a broken wrist and his with some serious damage to a calf or ankle.

Clement threw the metal pipe at the man he'd dropped, causing him to moan and curl up when it struck him in the chest. Cait's partner snarled, "Bastard. You're lucky I don't have time to give you more."

Cait asked, "Status on the target?"

Garrett said, "Not down here. I'm, uh, covering the escape route."

Clement laughed suddenly. "Bradley, you need more cardio in your life. I don't see him either. Morin?"

Sabrina replied, "He came out onto the fire escape. Heading up."

Cait bolted through the nearest doorway, coating herself in a shield of force magic in case an ambush awaited inside. Nothing impeded her progress, and she found the open back window that led out onto the metal balcony and attached stairs.

Sabrina asked, "Want me to take him down?"

Clement replied, "Do you have a clean shot, safe from civilians?"

"I do."

"Green light."

A moment later, the woman growled a curse. "Magical shield. I don't have anti-magic rounds loaded." After a short pause, she said, "The prick blew up my drone with a fireball. Outstanding."

Cait chuckled at the other woman's dark humor and pelted up the fire escape, switching magazines in her pistol. She focused on pushing more power into her shield as she emerged at the top, in case her quarry was lying in wait, ready to shoot her. That fear proved unfounded, and she spotted him as he vaulted from one building to the next in an all-out run. "Got us a track star up here."

Clement replied, "Hopefully your cardio is better than Bradley's." He sounded slightly out of breath himself.

Cait laughed. "A bit." She pumped the magic from her shield into her muscles, sinews, heart, and lungs now that she had the target in sight. The influx of power was one of the feelings she liked best in the world, almost as if only in those moments was she *fully* herself. The spring chill that had been noteworthy a moment before no longer intruded on her senses, and she dashed after the fleeing fugitive. She leapt easily over the gap between rooftops and shouted, "U.S. Marshals. Stop. You're under arrest."

He replied by spinning and throwing a fireball at her. She called up an inclined plane of force to deflect it upward, where it would hopefully dissipate and do no damage. She knew people who could suck in others' magical attacks, even use them to feed their own, which had always seemed like the optimal solution. Unfortunately, she lacked that ability.

Her belief that he'd stopped to fight turned out to be wrong. As the fireball moved out of her visual field, she saw him running again. He curled around a piece of HVAC equipment on the roof, breaking line of sight, and she pushed herself into a run. It took several more leaps and almost a full minute of pursuit before she was near enough to take useful action. *Bastard must be pumping himself up, too. Show-off.*

She lifted her pistol, not stopping her run, and pulled the trigger three times to dispatch rounds toward the rooftop at his feet. The angle was such that they ricocheted, one of them hitting him at least significantly enough to compel him into another spinning counterattack. That's what she'd hoped for. She summoned a force wall in his path as she dove to the side to avoid whatever he was about to attack her with. His lightning crackled around the space she'd occupied.

Cait had the perfect angle to watch the end-product of her attack as he spun back and ran face-first into the wall she'd put in his way. He rebounded, then stumbled and fell backward onto the rooftop. She ran over to him, ready to blast him with her lightning and send him into dreamland. Blood leaked from his broken nose, and his eyes fluttered, suggesting the impact with the wall had stunned or maybe concussed him.

She reached for the small pouch on the back of her belt that contained her handcuffs and used them to snap his hands together. She added some force restraints, putting bands around his knees and elbows, and held her gun loosely in her hand, ready in case he decided to try something stupid. "The anti-magic bullets were a good idea," she commented as Clement arrived at her side.

"Always nice to have around. So, I couldn't help noticing that you're a magical."

She flicked her gaze sideways but saw no condemnation or fear in his expression. "Yep."

He nodded. "Elf?"

"Witch."

The moment hung as she awaited his response. He broke into a grin. "Awesome. I've been telling Levitt we need magical support for ages."

Garrett's voice came through the speaker in her glasses, panting. "Everyone okay?"

She laughed. "Yeah. We got him."

"Excellent. Keane, you drink for free tonight."

Clement frowned. "Hey. Why her and not me? Trying to suck up already?"

"You didn't save me from falling to my death."

Their team leader laughed again. "Fair point. Okay, let's get this scumbag to lockup and celebrate our victory."

With a smile, Cait moved to assist him. *I think I'm gonna like it here.*

CHAPTER FOUR

The rest of the day had passed in a haze of paperwork. Cait hadn't gotten the chance to unload her cardboard box of belongings, only to power on her computer, set up her account, and get to work. It was amazing how much documentation the Marshals required whenever someone discharged a weapon, even when there were no fatalities.

It was after five when she finished, and she hung out for fifteen minutes while the others closed up shop. They escorted her to a bar a few blocks away, and she laughed when she saw that it was called The Shillelagh. Its hand-painted sign featured a gnarled wooden walking stick with a heavy handle serving as an underline to the name. As they entered, she asked, "Did you choose this on my account?"

Simon replied, "Nope. Believe it or not, this is our standard hangout. It does suggest that you're supposed to be here, Cait Keane." He added an Irish accent to her name, and she laughed again.

The inside was wood and brass, notably far from modern. She felt like she'd stepped into the distant past, the only false note the huge flat screens on either end of the long bar. which displayed football matches—soccer, in the States. The chairs around the bar were all occupied by men and women in suits or other business wear. A small row of tables ran along the right-hand wall, and the narrow front area opened into a wider room in the back, which held more tables. A couple of servers in black pants and green shirts circulated through the noisy crowd, taking orders and bantering with the customers.

Cait whispered, "Power above, power below, let it build, let it flow. Power around, power within, reveal to me my magical kin." Several people took on a hazy outline as her power searched for others with magical auras. The spell was standard upon entering a place she wasn't familiar with and for those she knew well, depending on the circumstances.

A couple of the patrons were magicals, and surprisingly, so was the bartender. The woman was tall and blonde, but nothing suggested she had magical abilities. *Still, it would be handy in that kind of job. Pacify the drunks with magic.*

Simon tapped her on the arm. "We'll follow the others upstairs in a minute. There's someone I'd like you to meet."

She realized that Garrett, Clement, and Sabrina had all continued into the back room, where presumably a staircase led to a second level. "Sure."

He escorted her to the far end of the bar, where a man in a suit smiled at their approach. He stood and extended a hand. Simon gripped it and said, "Paul Andrews, I'd like to introduce you to the newest member of my team. This is Cait Keane."

The other man shifted the hand in her direction, and she shook it. "A pleasure." He was tall and trim with brown hair. She probably wouldn't have noticed him in passing on the street. *Which might be a good quality for a spy type.*

Simon commented, "Don't count on that. Paulie here is the head of the local branch of the PDA."

Andrews scowled. "How many times have I asked you not to call me Paulie? I don't call you Simie."

Cait laughed. "Maybe you should start."

He turned a smile on her. "I try not to swim in the muck just because others choose to do so."

"Some would say that the Paranormal Defense Agency is always in the muck."

She put enough tease in the words to ensure he recognized the joke. He placed a hand on his chest. "Wounded. I'm wounded. We just met, and you strike such a wicked blow." He shook his head, then grinned. "Some would say the same about the Marshals. I heard about the rooftop takedown, by the way. Nice work. I especially liked the part where he ran into a magic wall."

Cait turned a surprised gaze on Simon, who nodded. "The PDA has lots of eyes in the sky here. Sort of a *1984* constant surveillance kind of thing."

Andrews gave a small sigh, and she recognized a familiar argument in it. "It's not all that. He's miffed because we won't let him have access to our information whenever he wants it."

She replied, "Why not? Aren't we all on the same side?"

He laughed. "Same side, sure. Same *team*, though, not so

much. You've got to give to get, and your boss here is pretty stingy."

Simon clapped him on the arm. "Always good to see you, Paul."

"You too, Simon." He climbed onto his stool and turned his attention back to the match.

Her chief shook his head and touched her shoulder, gesturing toward the back room. "He's a solid guy but a jerk. Not bad as far as PDA people like him go, but you can assume he's always working an angle."

They reached the stairs, and he led the way up them. She countered, "And you're not?"

His laugh sounded muffled because he was facing away from her but signaled genuine amusement. "Oh no, I'm a total jerk, too. You've got to be to have my job."

Several minutes went by fast as they placed drink orders with a server and organized a Boston Marshals' billiards tournament. The initial match was Simon versus Garrett, so she leaned against the wall next to Clement to watch. "You all do this often?"

He shrugged. "A couple of times a month, unless we have a reason to celebrate, like tonight." He grinned at her. "The capture, of course. Not your arrival."

Cait suppressed the desire to stick her tongue out at him. "Of course. How could it be any other way?"

"Right? Anyway, we don't always come here, although this is the primary watering hole for folks like us."

"It does have that law enforcement vibe."

He laughed. "True words. Once you know how LEO places feel, you can always recognize them."

They moved to a nearby standing table as the server

reappeared. Cait asked, "So, what can you tell me about Paul Andrews?"

"Ah, you got to meet our friend from the PDA. He's not bad. Little stiff. Untrusting. Probably untrustworthy. Typical federal suit."

She laughed. "Aren't we, or at least the chief, also typical federal suits?"

He accepted his Guinness from the server and took a sip before replying. "Arguably yes. But it's a continuum."

"Of federal suitness."

"Exactly." He winced and called, "Really, Garrett? You're supposed to sink the eight *last*. Do you still not understand the rules of this game?"

The man in question flipped him off, and Cait set down her drink, a local draft cider, and accepted the cue from him. She was facing off against Sabrina, and their match went quickly. Cait lost, fair and square, although she hadn't played up to her potential. Her focus was lacking after a long day filled with unexpected events.

She wandered over to where the other woman's drink awaited her on a table and sat in the chair across from her, nursing her cider. "Good game." She'd gotten a better look at Sabrina than on her first moments in the office and could now see the attractive lines of her face and the luster in her dark hair that spoke of careful attention. Her makeup was subtle but perfect. She had dark eyes that seemed somehow mysterious. *I could use a little mystery in my looks. Maybe I can get some tips.*

Sabrina shrugged. "I feel like you maybe weren't at your best."

Cait laughed. "Possibly. Even if I had been, I think you might have carried the day."

They were interrupted by a couple of guys who approached to talk to the other woman. She noted how Sabrina's attitude shifted at their approach, becoming open and friendly. Her voice was almost flirty as she chatted with them. The pair left after securing a promise that she'd visit their table before she departed.

When they were gone, the other woman's face fell back into a more neutral expression. Cait said, "You fit in well here."

Sabrina nodded. "Which is unexpected because of how I look and act the rest of the time, right?" The words could've sounded defensive, but that edge wasn't present, rendering it simply a recitation of facts. "I'm not all that good with people. It's like putting on a costume when I'm in this kind of situation."

She seemed reluctant to discuss it further, so Cait didn't push. "Well, it's an effective one."

Sabrina raised her glass in a toast, and Cait felt a tap on her arm. She turned to see Chief Levitt beside her. He said, "Come out onto the balcony with me."

Once outside, he led her to a corner and pulled out a pipe and a lighter from an inside pocket. She gazed down over the railing as he lit the tobacco, seeing only a narrow road and the fronts of other bars and restaurants on the opposite side of it. After he took a couple of puffs, he said, "You're having an eventful week."

She laughed. "Yeah, kind of. I traded the frying pan for the fire."

"Hotel room okay? Government rates don't get us too much."

"It's fine. I appreciate you setting it up."

He waved it off. "Since you transferred on such short notice, it was the least we could do. Along with honoring the time off requests you'd already had approved in Columbus."

"Still, I'm grateful."

After a pause filled with the aroma of tobacco smoke, he said, "So, tell me a little bit about your work with the Special Operations Group. How often do you wind up in the field?"

She leaned against the railing and sipped her drink. "No way to tell. We train a lot more than we deploy, of course, but there's no pattern. If the local branch can't handle something, we get called in. If you need me to, I can use vacation time for the long training sessions."

He shook his head. "It's all Marshals work, no need for that. But you're gonna cause me a lot of paperwork, Keane."

"My last chief said the same thing. Hopefully, you'll decide I'm worth it."

"I don't see any reason to doubt it." He puffed on his pipe with a look of momentary discomfort. "So, your secret didn't last long."

She stilled the impulse to take the neutral comment as a criticism. "I wasn't aware it was a secret?"

He laughed. "No, but I was unsure how to bring it up to the team. That problem pretty much solved itself, from what I hear, which is kind of nice for me, personally." His manner set her at ease.

Cait shrugged. "It was reflex. No thought, only action."

"And a good one. Especially for Garrett." He puffed a few times. "I've never had the opportunity to oversee a magical. Anything in particular I need to be aware of?"

She smiled. *I was in Columbus for years. My chief never asked that question. It's already better here.* "Nothing out of the ordinary, except you can expect that I'll occasionally be unreachable during time off. I'll let you know when."

He nodded, and his voice lowered slightly. "On Oriceran?"

Cait doubted he even realized what he'd done. *You weren't kidding when you said you don't have much experience around magicals, boss.* A rueful laugh escaped her. "No, a visit to the other planet would be a welcome vacation. I'll be with my family. They're too needy for relaxation."

He laughed and gestured with his pipe, pointing the mouthpiece at her. "Oh, if you think *yours* are needy, let me tell you about *mine*."

CHAPTER FIVE

The late night getting to know her new colleagues made the four o'clock morning alarm on her phone far more jarring than usual. Still, she forced herself out of bed, already wearing her training clothes, laced up her running shoes, and headed for the fitness center. The long-stay hotel that was her current home had a pretty good setup with several cardio machines and a decent array of free weights. She spent forty-five minutes interval training on the treadmill. When her workout was complete, she walked back to her room on rubbery legs, showered, and prepared to face the day.

That meant a pair of black pants, comfortable but professional boots, a dark blue blouse, and a stylish leather jacket. A shoulder holster rested underneath it, with her Glock 23 on the left and an extra magazine filled with thirteen anti-magic bullets on the right. She didn't carry a purse, so the wallet holding her badge and ID went into a small case at the back of her belt, along with a credit card and some cash. The pouch containing her cuffs was next to it. Finally, she checked to be sure the plastic clips that would hold her cell phone were in place on her left hip. The phone itself she slipped into the jacket's inner pocket.

She had stepped out of the front of the hotel and headed for Starbucks to grab the magical train to the coffee shop nearest the courthouse when her phone vibrated. She dug it out and answered, "Keane."

Clement's voice said, "Got a situation. Come to this address." She acknowledged, hung up, and summoned an autonomous car to take her there. On the way, she called up a map of the route, knowing she had a long way to go to achieve a full understanding of how Boston's geography worked. The destination was in the suburbs north of the city proper. Despite the car's impressive velocity, it still took almost twenty-five minutes to get there.

She instructed it to drop her off a block away because a police cordon had closed off the streets around the address she sought. She flashed her badge as she crossed the outer perimeter and ducked under the crime scene tape. The number of police cars was frankly impressive, and an ambulance stood by as well. They gave her a moment of hope before she noticed the coroner's truck parked behind it. *Well, this isn't going to be good.*

The house was large, on a long street of similarly attractive residences. She counted twelve windows in the front alone, across two floors, which suggested a goodly number of rooms. The landscaping was pristine, adding to her impression that whoever lived inside was wealthy, important, or both. Garrett met her at the door in response to her message letting the team know she'd arrived. He asked, "You have experience with crime scenes, right?"

She nodded. "Of course. Don't worry. I won't step on any clues."

"Good." The interior of the house was richly appointed but not ostentatious. Art that looked expensive hung on every wall, pieces that complemented each other in size, color, and theme.

She observed, "Someone with taste lives here."

Clement looked down from the top of a wooden switchback staircase and countered, *"Lived* here. Come on up."

Cait steeled herself against whatever surprises lay ahead. She'd been around death any number of times as part of her job, sometimes as the cause rather than a spectator. Still, she wasn't immune to the shock that came with having proof of life's precariousness set out like a warning in front of her. As she climbed toward Clement with Garrett behind her, she asked, "Why are we here?"

Garrett replied, "It's a judge." *Well, that explains that.*

The bedroom was large, clearly a master suite. A king-size bed with a dark blue comforter and a plethora of indulgent-looking pillows dominated the space, with nightstands on either side and a massive, curved video screen mounted on the opposite wall. The windows had sheer curtains beneath heavier ones that matched the bed covering.

On top of that dark cobalt duvet was a pale body. A male with messy gray hair, clad in only a pair of running shorts. More gray covered his chest, a notable amount of it, and she made an instinctive estimation of his age as early sixties. He wasn't out of shape, but neither was he fit, landing somewhere in that nebulous zone between them.

His arms and legs stuck out in a rigid approximation of da Vinci's Vitruvian man, making him seem alive even though his pallor and stillness made it clear that train had left the station some time before.

Her gaze climbed reluctantly up to his face, which held an expression of horror, his mouth gaping open and his eyes locked wide. She forced cool neutrality into her tone. "Doesn't look like a happy way to go. What killed him?"

A voice from her left surprised her, and she realized the figure on the bed had so captured her attention that she'd missed the fact that multiple police officers were present. She further noted that an EMT whose services certainly wouldn't be needed was at hand, standing beside someone in a windbreaker with white letters spelling Coroner, whose skills probably would. The latter, a sandy-haired middle-aged man in dark clothes, replied, "Don't know. He's got a force field or something on him. We can't get in to find out. Waiting on our magical support."

The rasp of a throat clearing came from her right, and she looked over to see Chief Levitt at the opposite side of the room, talking with a man whose suit quality suggested he was likely a detective. *Come on, Cait, get your head out of your ass and into the game.* "Let me see what I can do."

She moved closer to the bed, careful to step only where other treads were visible on the plush beige carpet. She whispered, "Magic to hurt, magic to heal, all magic around, now reveal." The body glowed in her shifted senses, showing proof of the magic coating him. Her gaze slid systematically across the room, searching for other magics that might be clues or dangers, but found none. "Agreed, magic."

Cait closed her eyes and murmured another spell. "Be it water or fire, air or land, a single caster, or more than one hand; the nature of this magic, help me understand." Her power reached out to investigate the nature of the other magic in the room. She examined it slowly and methodically, detecting force magic at work, then realized what had happened with as much certainty as if she'd seen it.

She opened her eyes, and the pressure of the discovery lessened as her magical senses faded. "He suffocated. The caster tightened the shield until he couldn't breathe."

Sounds of surprise and anger came from around the room. Levitt's voice was tight as he asked, "Can you remove it?"

"Yes."

"Do it."

Before she could obey, a uniformed officer protested that such an action would violate their crime scene. Clement calmly told him to shut the hell up and suggested that if he had a real problem with it, he could come to the courthouse and make his case in front of one of the judge's colleagues. The officer sighed like he had something more to say but didn't respond.

Cait walked over to the body, put her hand six inches above his foot, and extended her power again. As she drew the lines of his figure with her hovering palm, chanting, the shield fell away under her fingers. She frowned as she came to a further realization about the magic.

"This was more than a barrier. It also had sharp points stabbing into him, penetrating his muscles. His arms and legs initially locked that way from the pain of the spell. The power only held it in place."

She stepped away when the body was free of its magical bonds to allow the detectives and coroner access to examine it. Her careful steps took her over to Garrett's side. Her colleague seemed to know most of the people in the room, and she'd noted him conversing with several of them while she worked. "They have anything?"

He shook his head with a frown. "No evidence at all, beyond the fact that it was a magical."

Cait replied, "Or someone who hired a magical. No telling how many of them were in here when it went down. Random, do you think?"

He let out a dark laugh. "This kind of damage, I doubt it." She nodded. That was her conclusion as well. He gestured for her to follow, and they stepped out into the hallway and walked a dozen feet away. He put his phone on speaker and hit a button. A familiar female voice replied, "Primo pizza, where every single bite has pepperoni, or you get a free stick of pepperoni."

Guess I see why you left the room first. That wouldn't have played well in there. Her partner snorted. "What do you have, Sabrina?"

She said, "Judge Gideon Meyer. In Boston for twenty years in his current job. Other courts around the country before that. Kind of a nomad."

Cait muttered, "That could complicate things a bit."

Garrett nodded as Sabrina continued, "I didn't find much more than that on the magical dark web, either. Some complaints that he might have been overly harsh on magicals who came before him, particularly infomancers. But really, you'll have that with any judge." *She's an infomancer. Good to have that confirmed.*

Garrett asked, "Close relatives?"

She replied, "A wife who's out of town but on her way home now, and a kid who's a graduate student in both mechanical and electrical engineering at MIT."

Cait said, "Guess I know where we're heading next."

CHAPTER SIX

She'd assumed it would be her and Garrett heading over to the Massachusetts Institute of Technology, but instead Clement was at her side, behind the wheel of a recent year Dodge Charger. The engine maintained its raspy rumble as he pushed the car, foot rarely leaving the accelerator, disdaining the use of the brake until she was positive they would wind up in a horrific crash with some unsuspecting vehicle. But his piloting skills were adequate to the task as he wove through main avenues and side streets, presumably in the direction of the university's campus. "You've memorized the map?"

He laughed. "I've been here for years. Got it down solid. Survival skill."

"Color me jealous. I had Columbus in my head like that, finally, right about the time I left."

He spun the wheel and the car's rear fishtailed a little as it forced itself back in line. "You'll get it. Until then, I'll do the driving."

She laughed. "When I do, can I drive this?"

He snorted. "No one drives my baby unless they're a blood relative or I'm trying to get them into bed. You offering?"

She rolled her eyes and gave a deadpan response. "Yes. Oh yes. You're such an incredibly, irresistibly, manly man. My desperately inadequate feminine restraint is completely overwhelmed."

Clement expelled a barked laugh. "That's what all the girls say, yet I'm still single. Makes no sense at all." The self-deprecating humor earned him points. "Anyway, get ready to flash your badge." He pulled up to a guard post and security came to both windows.

Cait showed her ID, he did the same, and they waited while the guards verified their credentials over their radios. "Why the concern? It's only college, right?"

They got their wallets back, and the gate in front of them rose as the tire spikes in the pavement retracted. They rolled through, and he replied, "Tons of important stuff going on here. Government research, startups, and scientists redefining the bleeding edge of technology on a daily basis. Hell, I think even NASA has some people here."

She frowned. "Seems as if it would be fairly easy to infiltrate. Apply, get accepted, come to school here."

Clement pulled into a loading zone and threw a "Marshals" placard on the dash, then climbed out of the vehicle. Once she'd done the same, he replied, "I don't think getting in is quite that simple. Probably lots of layers of background checks, including a look by the government. But you're right. I bet this place is less secure than the folks running it might believe."

Cait paced beside him down a sidewalk that ran around

the perimeter of an open common area. The bright sun overhead had raised the temperature sufficiently that students were hanging out on the grass, although she was still glad for her jacket. "Is that something we should be concerned with?"

He shrugged. "We have to worry about everything, don't we?" It was true. Their mandate extended in all sorts of unlikely directions, some of which might cross university grounds.

She changed the subject. "Where's our target?"

"Lab building four, dead ahead."

"They have four lab buildings?" Her college, a big state university, only had three during her time there.

Clement laughed. "They have nine."

Cait sighed. "Going to have to do some serious research on the area."

"Sounds like you've got a *really* fun weekend ahead of you."

They entered through oversized double doors and again faced security, along with metal, magic, and explosive detectors. They reaffirmed their credentials and passed through the cordon, then climbed the stairs to the second level.

While the exterior had been undistinguished, the interior was clean and modern-looking with light-colored tile floors under their feet and soft lighting overhead. White walls with many doors formed a long central hallway that extended to the building's full depth. She remarked, "Sterile."

Clement nodded. "No distractions, I guess. I think I'd lose my mind in a place like this."

Cait laughed. "Yeah, I'm with you on that one." They found the lab they were looking for—number 4127—knocked, and entered. It was a modest rectangle, narrow to the left and right and longer toward the building's edge. Tools and components covered two large metal tables.

Behind the far one stood a tall, trim figure with blonde hair and oversized goggles, creating sparks as she touched the cylindrical tool in her hand to pieces of unrecognizable equipment on the surface. After a moment, the woman registered their presence, pulled off her goggles, and shook out her hair. "Can I help you?"

"Kendra Meyer?" Clement replied.

"Yeah, that's me."

He said, "We're Deputy US Marshals Austin and Keane." He gestured as he spoke so she could connect the name to the person. "I'm sorry to be the bearer of dire news, but your father was found dead this morning."

Cait had delivered similar information on a few occasions, both as marshal and as a member of her magical community, and it was never easy. This one wasn't as bad as most since instead of breaking down, screaming, or responding with denial, Kendra sighed and nodded sadly. "How did it happen?"

She replied, "Someone killed him."

The woman's reaction to *that* information had been more forceful, bringing forth anger and nearly overwhelming grief. She'd invited them to her office and now busied herself making coffee, the dispenser filling paper cups for them and a mug for her. She handed them off, then sat behind her desk and sipped quietly.

They did the same, content to give her the time she needed to compose herself. Finally, Kendra sat upright and met their eyes. *You can almost see her putting on her scientist persona, shutting the personal stuff away.* "Okay. Give me the details."

Clement replied, "He missed a breakfast meeting, which was atypical enough that the person waiting for him called the police for a safety check. They found him."

Cait continued, "He was killed by magic. Suffocated." She didn't offer any more details, nor did she try to soften the blow by suggesting his death probably came fast. Given the pain of the magical invasion of his flesh, no matter how rapid it was on the outside, it would've felt much longer on the inside. *She doesn't need to know that.*

Kendra nodded. "Did you catch whoever did it?"

Clement shook his head, showed them that his phone was now in recording mode, and set it on the desk. "Not yet, which is why we're here. We hoped you could give us some insight."

"I'll try. Whatever I can do." Her voice quivered a little.

Cait asked, "Did he have any enemies?"

The other woman burst out in pained laughter, dark and cold. "All of them. He put away people from the Roses and the Dragons. He had no friends in Boston."

She stored the names to ask about later and pretended to understand. "Okay, any specific cases involving magicals that you're aware of?"

The discussion continued for fifteen minutes, but the daughter had nothing more to share that seemed like a solid lead. They offered their condolences and headed out when the woman ran out of words, her emotions finally getting the better of her. Once they were back in the car, Cait asked, "The Roses and the Dragons?"

Clement nodded as he pressed the button to start the engine. "Boston is home to several criminal enterprises, some large, some small, some smart, some dumb, some ambitious, some petty. The two biggest are the Roses and the Dragons. They each claim half the town, more or less, and the smaller groups make arrangements with them for permission to operate and protection from the others. Things have been quiet with them for almost a year, as best as I know from people who watch over them. They've never been stupid enough to cross our path before."

Cait nodded. "Guess there's a first time for everything."

"Yeah." He backed the car out and turned it toward the exit.

She tapped her phone to activate it. "Who should I call to arrange a meeting?"

He chuckled. "Don't bother. I'll have someone back at the office do it. Setting up a chat will take a while since they like to delay investigators on principle. We'll start the process." Clement looked over and grinned. "Better spend the weekend resting up. Next week's going to be busy."

"This one wasn't?"

"Welcome to Boston, Keane."

CHAPTER SEVEN

Cait had spent the rest of that Friday doing more paperwork and chasing down leads that went nowhere. A short nap followed a quick meal at a South Indian restaurant on the way home. She woke up to her alarm in the middle of the night, changed into jeans and a t-shirt with her most comfortable leather jacket over it, and grabbed the duffel bag she always kept packed for trips home. A whispered incantation and a gesture summoned a portal connecting her hotel room in Boston to the backyard of her family's house in Ireland.

She stepped through onto an engraved stone circle in the corner nearest the house and into the morning sunlight. Two red-haired women emerged from the back door, heading toward her. She smiled at the sight of her sisters and moved to greet them.

The small community of witches and their families was south of Westport, on the western side of the Emerald Isle. To the west of the village, Croagh Patrick rose toward the sky, but she couldn't see it through the thick trees that surrounded their neighborhood. Her family's house, like the others in the small village, had been crafted by magic to fit together seamlessly.

The place was centuries old, and power radiated in it, through it, and around it. Magic was inherent to their village life, substituting for what technology accomplished in other places. Her older sibling Brianna was the first to arrive. Bigger and stronger than she was, her sister had curly red hair Cait envied and a wide smile. She held the large kitchen knife she'd brought with her to the side as she wrapped Cait in a hug. "About time you got here."

She snorted. "Overslept a little. You know, it is the middle of the night in Boston."

Brianna stepped back and gave her a light punch on the shoulder. Light for Brianna, that was. It still knocked Cait back half a step. "Excuses, always excuses with you." She laughed and feinted a punch of her own, but her sister lifted an eyebrow and shook her head. "And weak."

Her other sibling, Aisling, stepped forward for her embrace. "Shut up, Bri. Everyone's weak compared to you body-wise, and you're weak compared to everyone brain-wise."

Her older sister laughed at the comment from her younger one. "Whoa. Sick burn, Aisling. College is helping you."

Cait whispered loudly, "Let's wait until she falls asleep and dump cold water on her head." Aisling squeezed her harder but didn't reply, only stepped back. Brianna spent her time working for the good of the community, overseeing the shared needs of the coven as a whole.

Aisling was training to become a technomancer, her

skills in science almost as prodigious as her abilities with magic. She attended Trinity College, Dublin, and would finish up this year as long as she kept focused. *Which, in this family, can be a bit of a challenge.* Cait walked away from the house and wandered through the backyard as her siblings continued to bicker. The early plants in the garden were doing well, and the fruit bushes and trees also realized it was spring and showed a little more life.

She turned to her sisters. "Everything looks good back here. You two aren't totally useless at growing food, after all." It was a standing family joke. When they'd been younger, gardening had been her particular responsibility. Since becoming adults, they shared the tasks of growing and gathering food.

Aisling scowled theatrically. "I'm telling Mom that you're being a jerk." She ran for the door, and Cait dashed after her and tackled her into the grass, both of them laughing as they wrestled, trying to pin the other. Finally, Brianna intervened, pulling Aisling off Cait's chest, where she'd been holding her down and tickling her ruthlessly.

Cait caught her breath and climbed to her feet. "You don't fight fair."

Although she'd been talking about Aisling, Brianna replied, "There are no fair fights. If you let it be fair, you're halfway to lost."

Cait rolled her eyes. "Thank you, oh wise champion of the coven." Brianna flipped her off, and she laughed. "Now the homecoming is complete."

From beyond the door Aisling had opened, her mother's voice called, "Not quite. Get in here, girls."

Cait obeyed and went straight for the kitchen, where

her mother wrapped her in a hug, squeezing her like she hadn't seen her for years, even though it had only been a couple of weeks. She said, muffled, "Suffocating." The joking word sent a chill through her as she thought about the judge, and she pushed that thought away. *Work time is for work. Family time is for family.*

She escaped her mother's clutches and regarded the woman. "You're still the most *go halainn* witch in the village, Mom." The years had deepened her beauty, rather than damaging it, dark red waves of hair framing a pale face with hazel eyes that matched hers.

Moira laughed. "Flatterer."

"Does it get me a treat?"

Her mother gestured at a plate to her left. "Fresh blueberry muffins. Have some."

The kitchen was the largest room in the house. The first floor also featured a small dining room and a living area, with the upper level taken up by bedrooms. Both floors had bathrooms and storage and all the other requisite needs. The lights were magical. The abundant arcane energy kept them burning with minimal effort on their parts.

Magic provided the water pressure. Heat and cooling were magical. Enticing the crops to grow was magical. Power was part and parcel of daily life in the village, and being there refreshed her—body and soul.

Together, they gathered and prepared food for an early lunch—vegetable soup thick with potatoes, onions, and carrots, with a loaf of freshly baked bread, butter, and honey. They sat around the rectangular table in the dining room, which was large enough to hold a couple more.

Their father was notably absent, although Cait knew he had planned a trip to Oriceran. His work as an archaeologist took him there often, with unpredictable return times, and he always had the best tales when he did rejoin them in the village.

They traded stories and updated one another on their lives as they ate, over much laughter and a few snarky jibes. A knock at the door came as a surprise, and her mother called, "Please enter."

A girl came through the door, the youngest child of the coven's leader. "My mother told me to tell you there will be a coven meeting this evening, and she needs you to attend."

Her mother inclined her head. "Of course, I'll be there. Thank you for letting me know. Would you like a muffin?"

The girl's serious expression split with a grin. "Oh, definitely yes."

Brianna laughed and held out the plate. "Take two. Cait doesn't want to have another one."

The girl obliged, and when she left, loudly banging the door closed behind her, Cait asked, "Why don't I want another muffin, exactly? I kind of thought I did, to be honest."

Her older sister grinned. "Because there's plenty of time before the meeting."

"Time for what?"

"Training."

CHAPTER EIGHT

After lunch, Cait climbed the stairs to her small bedroom and pulled off her jeans and t-shirt. She replaced them with a pair of martial arts pants, a plain black tee, and a *gi*, a martial arts top, all in black. Light training shoes, not heavy enough to slow her down but sufficient to prevent foot injuries, completed the outfit.

She emerged from her room as Brianna, who wore a similar outfit although more worn, did the same. Her sister pointed out the disparity, and Cait shrugged. "Not all of us can have the idyllic life of living at home and training all the time."

Her older sibling laughed. "Yeah, it's tough. But someone needs to do the things that need doing. You don't think Mom wants to make the walk into town every day for supplies and haul them back here, do you?"

"We have portals for that."

"We don't like to draw that much attention. Living in the city has made you soft."

Cait laughed and shook her head. *Yeah, soft, that's what I am. You should come play on my field sometime. Then we'll see who's soft and who's not.* "Whatever. Let's go."

They crossed the open oval area in the center of the houses on a path they had taken many times before. She and her sisters had trained with Delsanra since they were old enough to walk. Most of the coven members and their families did too, but as Brianna had pointed out, some embraced it more than others. Cait had been near the more active end of that scale before she left for the States, and she still made a point of finding time for combat training on at least every other visit to her home village.

When they reached the opposite side, they walked through the narrow, grassy area separating one house from the next into their teacher's backyard. Delsanra was a wizard who used a nontraditional wand, like hers, in the form of a bracelet. Unlike her, he wore his on his left wrist since for him, magic was rarely a primary method of attack. Hers was on the right because she was more dexterous with that hand, and at moments like her plummet after Garrett in the apartment building, every advantage mattered.

He was dressed in similar clothes to theirs, although his tunic wasn't tied closed but rather hung open, revealing glimpses of tanned skin and lean muscles as he moved through his practice forms. Her brain always thought of water when she watched his combat style due to how his movements flowed from one to another as if not by choice, but because that's the way the world wanted them to go. Also like water, they were fierce and irresistible.

He gripped an engraved stick in each hand, intricate designs in green on black wood. She knew he saw imaginary opponents, blocking or redirecting their blows, dancing away from them entirely or counterstriking. His head snapped from side to side occasionally as if addressing a new threat. His movements carried him in all directions, but he always knew the limits of his practice space, and his motions brought him back toward the middle whenever he neared an edge.

After watching him for a minute, she was broken from her reverie when an object gently struck her arm. She turned to find Brianna extending a walking stick with a carved knob on the top to her, holding a similar weapon in her other hand. Hers was a little longer than the one she offered Cait. She took the shillelagh with a nod and circled away from her sister. When they were both in position, Brianna met her gaze, and they attacked simultaneously.

Delsanra's motions didn't speed up or become more forceful as he shifted from imaginary threats to tangible ones. She whipped her club in a horizontal slash, aiming for his shoulder. He bent and spun, letting it pass easily above him. The move took him closer to Brianna, who was already bringing her weapon down in a vertical strike. He parried, wood cracking against wood, and used his other stick to smack Brianna on the hip, none too gently.

As her sister backed off, Cait pressed, whipping her club through a figure eight and stabbing it forward at her teacher's face. He brought his sticks up in an "X" to block the blow, then snapped a kick into her stomach that seemed gentle as it came in but propelled her several steps back and stole her breath.

He called, "Enough," and everyone froze. She bowed to him, and he returned it, then repeated the process with her sister. Turning back to her, Delsanra said with mild judgment, "Caitriona, you have not been keeping up your practice."

Cait sighed. Aside from her parents and one other person, only he regularly used her full name, and it always sounded like she was in trouble. "Busy, very busy."

He tilted his head to the side. "You know that no excuse is adequate, ever. Combat practice is preparation not only for *troid* but for life." She straightened, knowing what was coming next before he said it. "Brianna, demonstrate."

Her sister grinned and stalked toward the center of the yard. With a roll of her shoulders and a sense of anticipation, Cait matched her. They raised their weapons in a salute to one another, holding them vertically in front of their faces, then shifted into ready positions. This was familiar territory since she and her sister had been fighting and training together seemingly forever.

She knew the other woman would lead with an aggressive attack, and she fell back before it when it arrived. Her primary choice in fights of this kind was evasion, her secondary deflection, and she only committed to an outright block when no other option remained. Trying to fight her sister strength-to-strength was a losing strategy since Brianna was one of the strongest people she knew and annoyingly, didn't sacrifice much in speed or nimbleness in exchange.

As their long sticks smacked against each other and they threw punches and kicks that were dodged or opposed, she realized that her teacher was right. Her skills had atrophied. *Well, hell, where am I supposed to practice, my hotel room?* In Columbus, she'd rented a small house with a backyard that had given her a place to undertake her daily forms. *Although, if I'm being honest, I wasn't as diligent about it there as I could have been, either.*

After an even dozen exchanges that accomplished little beyond knocking some rust off her skills and earning her a bruise on her thigh where Brianna caught her with a good smash, Delsanra yelled, "Magic." The rules of practice were always that one started without that "crutch," as their teacher referred to it.

Cait tossed her stick to her left hand, where it became a secondary consideration to the use of her magic. Her sister wore a bracelet in place of her wand as well, on her off hand, like Delsanra. They threw bolts of force at one another and used that same power to block strikes from clubs. In this arena, Cait was slightly more skilled than her sister, having long used magic to counter the other woman's greater strength.

She managed to deflect Brianna's shillelagh far enough away to create an opening, used a modified form of lightning to generate a bright light that forced her sister to recoil involuntarily, and landed a kick directly in her stomach that caused her to stumble backward. Brianna crouched defensively, holding her club in guard position as she blinked and shook her head to clear her vision, but it was still a telling hit. Had she been able to pursue it, she would've had a good shot at taking down her opponent.

However, her teacher again called a halt. "Very good, both of you. Now, we will practice something a little different." They lined up next to each other, across from him, and he shook his head. "Brianna, I'm going to work with Caitriona. You watch and learn. We will work together on the same thing tomorrow." Her sister gave a slight frown of disappointment but stepped backward obligingly.

Cait saluted her teacher and shifted her weapon to her left hand when he indicated that magic would be part of the battle. They circled carefully, and he said, "Using the burst of light against your sister was a good technique. We're going to build on that instinct. Rather than using magic as a direct weapon or defense, it can also be very effectively used as a distraction to open other opportunities."

She nodded, not entirely sure what he meant. He made a quick move to her left, but as she turned to follow his motion, she caught something in her peripheral vision on the opposite side. She snapped up a shield in that direction, and he struck her with his club, knocking her weapon from her grasp. He said, "Now actually look over there."

She complied and saw that he had created an unfinished image of a person, solid enough to capture part of her attention. She scowled. "Tricky."

Delsanra lifted an eyebrow. "And, as some portion of your mind is no doubt saying, unfair. But we do not concern ourselves with fairness. Once you have chosen to fight, the only consideration is victory."

Cait smiled inwardly at the degree to which he echoed her sister's earlier comment and extended a hand, using her force magic like telekinesis, summoning the club back to it.

He instructed, "Keep your instincts open. Your eyes, your ears, and your magical senses. Pay attention to what they are *all* telling you, rather than relying on one more than the other."

They continued their slow combat, and as they moved along, she took fewer hits as she succumbed to his illusions less frequently. Then he changed his magic, sending small bursts of force at her legs to trip her or compel her to dodge. Both happened, and she paid for it with smacks from his weapon. By the end, she was half-exhausted and half-enraged, her frustration at not being able to easily deal with his seemingly minimal attacks brimming over.

Finally, Delsanra called a halt, laughing. "Cait, you have done well, but clearly, we have reached an ending point for you. These are not easy lessons to master. You should not expect success in one session." She sighed, and frustration flowed out of her. He had used those words with her often, and he was always correct.

She nodded and bowed respectfully. "Thank you, Delsanra. I'll find opportunities to practice to give a better account of myself next time."

He inclined his head. "I believe we'll see you no later than next week."

Cait frowned. "Why do you think that?"

He gestured at the sky. "Say that a little bird told me." As if on cue, she noticed sounds of chirping from the forest. Doubtless, they'd been there all along, but the timing was perfect. Her teacher looked at Brianna with a smile. "Now, the two of you spar again. Cait, show your sister what you've learned."

Brianna grinned, raised her shillelagh, and rushed at her.

CHAPTER NINE

A shower had soothed some, but not all, of her bruises and sore muscles and left Cait promising herself she would find a way to practice more to avoid ever feeling this level of soreness again. *Maybe there's a mixed martial arts gym or something I can sign up for.* She sat cross-legged on her bed and gave herself five minutes to meditate, bringing her disordered thoughts into some semblance of control. That allowed her to summon what little reserves of brainpower and will she had remaining after a night—and to be honest, several weeks—of not enough sleep.

The need for rest was one of the things that drew her home on a regular basis. Fortune or design had provided her with the ability to spend a couple of hours in quiet meditation on Croagh Patrick and become as rested as if she'd gotten enough sleep during the previous weeks. She was devoutly looking forward to that feeling. *Unfortunately, duty before pleasure as always.*

Cait pulled a pair of comfortable leather pants from the wooden wardrobe in the corner of her simple room, the only furniture it held other than a bed that was barely sufficient to hold her now that she was grown. The comforter covering it was handmade, as were the clothes she was slipping on.

A long top made of black silk embroidered in blue and red was the centerpiece of her look, extending from shoulders to calves and slit from the waist down. She swished back and forth simply to feel it move, and a memory of doing the same thing in a similar outfit when she was a child brought a smile to her lips.

She slid on a pair of high boots that ended just below her knees, then sat on the edge of the bed and methodically laced them up. Craftspeople in Westport had made the pants and footwear, and the shirt was a family heirloom. She looked at herself in the mirror mounted on the inside door of the wardrobe, grabbed a brush and ran it through her still damp hair, then pronounced it adequate and headed downstairs.

Twilight had fallen some time before, and the village was lit by magical orbs strung along the fronts of each house, creating a long horseshoe around the clearing. Only the part where the forest encroached lacked light. People wandered toward the darker center, individually, as couples, or as families. The coven's witches created an inner circle, sitting cross-legged with the other community members a row behind.

Her mother remained standing and when the motion had mostly ceased, intoned, "Sisters, let us call the elements to illuminate our discussion." The ritual words were instructions for them to pair up with the person on their left to cast dual magic. One witch cast fire and the other formed a cube of force to encase the flame. Then, together, they used their power to send the orbs flying ten feet overhead to create a glow around the gathering. Moira bowed her head, said in appreciation, "*Go raibh maith agat*," and took her seat.

All the eyes of the coven, including Cait's, went to a trio of witches across the circle from her. Sinead, a woman a decade older than her mother, and her two daughters, Eve and Nessa, rose to their feet. The three women were the coven's current leaders and had done a good job of it, in Cait's opinion. The daughters were older than her and her sisters, so they hadn't had all that much interaction in the past. In general, Cait categorized the trio as "fine." They had been a steady force, preserving the coven's status quo during their time as leaders.

Sinead said, "First, I'd like to congratulate you all. We've surveyed the gardens, and it appears we will be blessed with good growth and eventually a bountiful harvest. This is due to your wonderful work in planting and nurturing. You should have pride in what you have accomplished already and what it shall become."

A murmur of affirmation rippled around the group. "Second, we have received word from Westport of a new metalsmith joining the community. He specializes in intricate things like watches, jewelry, and other complicated mechanisms. Should you find that interesting or appealing, he has already indicated he will treat anyone from our coven as a valued customer."

Cait winced inwardly at the mixture of old-school and modern-day rattled off so close together. In general, any merchant in Westport with half a brain would reach out to the coven and offer them discounts or preferred status. Her reverie was interrupted as Sinead's eyes turned to her, and she smiled. "With us tonight is Caitriona. It is always good to see you when you return to visit."

The smile on the woman's face seemed forced, and Cait's instincts pricked up. *What have I done to you, wench?*

Sinead drew a deep breath, then sighed it out. "I am extremely happy and deeply sad to share the news that my two oldest children intend to leave the community." Murmurs and a few gasps around the circle answered her words, not because of the news itself, but for what it foretold for the coven.

"Eve will be heading to France in pursuit of a career. Nessa and her partner have decided they will make their home together in Dublin rather than here." That decision, which had been hanging in the air for a year and a half since Nessa had wed her wizard love, had been the source of some continuing gossip. The news that both daughters were leaving was something else entirely.

Sinead nodded as if she heard the unspoken questions. "As we all know, this means that I, and my family, can no longer serve as the *ceannairí* of the coven. There must be three, and it will only be Erin and me after." More mumbles went around, and Sinead raised a hand with a smile. "It is important for you to know that I, however, am going nowhere. I will be here to support whoever is selected to lead."

She dropped the hand. "Although it is a moment of transition, remember, things that do not change, die. This is true of our community as well as those in it. That growth sometimes comes with pain." She smiled at her daughters with a hint of sadness. “But we must endure it to continue on our chosen paths.” She flashed a grin. “Plus, one can hope for grandchildren soon.” Nessa rolled her eyes as the group laughed.

Sinead gestured up. “When the moon shines down on us in full, seven days from now, we will choose our new leaders. Go now and discuss with those closest to you who you might wish that to be.”

Cait followed her sisters and mother back into the house, where they poured cups of herbal tea and sat around the table. Brianna said, “They’ve been in charge a long while. I don’t even remember the last time this happened.”

Her mother nodded. “You were all young, and we didn’t include you in the discussion. As Sinead urged, households will discuss the coven's future and who they believe would be the best choice to lead them through it. Next, they’ll talk to other families and see where interests converge and diverge. Finally, gentle questions will determine who is willing to serve. Then the lines will form, and we will meet to find consensus.”

Aisling said, “You’ll get asked, Mom. Will you accept it?”

She shrugged. “That’s up to you all. There must be three, and it’s always the oldest.”

Brianna replied, “Hell yes. Let’s do it.”

Aisling laughed and shrugged. “You know I’ll support whatever you choose to do.”

Cait frowned, not wanting to be forced to make the decision. “You understand, I can’t move back here.”

Her mother nodded. “Since we also have Aisling, who

can fill in as needed to represent you, it won't be a problem as long as you can come when called."

She sighed and drummed her fingers on the table. Her mother's expression was neutral, but she saw the excitement on Aisling's face, and possibilities glimmered in Brianna's eyes. *Plus, my mother and sisters will make excellent leaders for the community.* "Okay. I'm in."

CHAPTER TEN

As the others cleaned up downstairs in preparation for sleep, Cait headed back to her room to change clothes again. The leather pants stayed, but she switched into hiking boots and pulled on a comfortable t-shirt with a sweater. She added a leather jacket, knowing it would be colder on Croagh Patrick. So equipped, she exited the house and whispered the spells to enhance her magical senses and regular ones.

She started forward, moving through the forest, her improved vision easily picking out the path, her ears noting the presence of animals but finding none of them a threat. She never performed this ritual armed, and everything she wore was handmade from items found in nature. To do otherwise reduced the effectiveness of whatever magic allowed her meditation to work as it did, something she'd learned only through long trial and error.

Cait reached the mountain and started upward, green glowing sigils, invisible to non-magicals, guiding her up the path that only her coven used. Most others approached

Croagh Patrick from the north, where a road ran up to its base. Catholic tourists were frequent, visiting the site where they believed St. Patrick had rid Ireland of snakes and venomous creatures.

After almost an hour of walking, she arrived at the top. The uneven surface was a mixture of large boulders and patches of thick grass, seemingly arranged at random. It looked out over the water in one direction and the forest in all others except where Westport's lights sparkled to the northeast.

She walked to one side, where wood lay stacked for visitors to use. She chuckled, knowing that one of the many chores Brianna performed for the coven was making sure the firewood stayed stocked here and there. The practice had the benefit of removing dead trees to create room for the still-growing ones to thrive.

Cait moved through the clearing and replaced some of the stones that had fallen over in the three separate rings of rocks on the mount, which were as far apart as space permitted on the mountain's top level. Tourists were generally respectful of the place, but sometimes, by accident or intent, they disturbed the ward circles.

The one closest to her village was her favorite, and she stepped inside, placing three logs in the center. She walked along the inner perimeter, her magical senses reaching out to ensure it was intact. Then she knelt, resting her weight on her heels and placing her hands on her thighs, and focused her mind. Her talent for substituting meditation for sleep was unique among her family and the coven as far as she knew. However, the only place where it functioned properly was here, on Croagh Patrick.

She'd tried it on other mountains, the village, and the States. It worked somewhat in all those places, and her meditation would equal twice as much sleep as the time she invested.

Here, among the ancient stones and the power they contained, she could make up for two weeks of short nights in only a couple of hours. She reached out with her right hand and waved it in an arcane gesture. "Connigh."

The wards came to life. They would prevent anything from entering the circle. Had she worn something plastic or unnatural into the ring, it would've lessened its protective ability.

Then she waggled her fingers at the logs. Fire stretched across the space between them, lighting them where they rested in a stone bowl hewn from the mountain rock. With a deep, centering breath, she pushed her thoughts inward and allowed herself to disconnect from the world around her.

Nine nines later, or eighty-one minutes for those unversed in her coven's magic rituals, she returned to consciousness. Her magical senses immediately noted a presence nearby. When she opened her eyes, she spotted a ghostly apparition in the shape of a fox pacing outside her wards. She felt pressure on her mind as it expressed its desire to enter, gently but firmly conveying a sense of impatience and importance.

She cast a spell to permit it to cross the boundary unharmed, then sealed the ward again, this time adjusting it so her new companion could depart at will. He sat before her and bowed his head in acknowledgment of her choice. When he spoke, his voice was somewhat insubstantial, coming across as a mix of words and wind, yet she understood him easily. "It is a moment of change for your coven."

She nodded. "It is. Our affairs draw the notice of the spirit world?"

His muzzle stretched sideways in a fox's version of a smile. "We are all one reality. Choices echo throughout it. Your decision will influence events already in motion."

She frowned, unsure if he meant her personal choices, that of her community, or maybe all of humanity. "Can you tell me what those events are?"

The fox shook its head. "I'm sorry. It is not given to me to reveal that information."

"I understand."

"What I may say is that you will need strength, wisdom, and above all, love to persevere through what is to come."

Sounds exactly like my mother. Could be it's her purpose to lead the coven at this time of oncoming challenge. "Thank you for your advice. I will pass it on to my family." He remained silent. One of the logs in the fire shifted position, sending embers spiraling up to the sky. After a time, she asked, "Is there something else?"

He nodded. "There is. It is unclear whether I should share it with you at this time."

"Because of the events?"

"Because of the danger involved."

Cait straightened and gazed across with serious eyes. "If you are able, I would like to hear, regardless of what it is."

His head lowered in a slow nod. "You will be called and will need support."

"The leaders of the coven?"

"No. You. Caitriona, daughter of Moira."

A chill trickled along her spine. "Could you explain what you mean by support?"

The fox rose to its feet, clearly preparing to depart. "I have told you all I can, for now. Return to the mountain at the next dark. You will be guided to your destination."

As he turned and padded away, she called, "Thank you," after him. She stood, mulling over the fact that while she knew he had said "destination," she had nonetheless heard "destiny" within it. *And here I thought getting a new job and potentially dealing with fighting criminal organizations was the difficult part of my life.* She shook her head, extinguished the fire, and walked back toward the village.

CHAPTER ELEVEN

Cait returned to her house in the early morning hours of Sunday, with the family still asleep overhead. The next hour was spent in the backyard, working through combat forms, practicing unarmed rather than weapon fighting. She focused on keeping her breathing even, flowing with the rippling breeze that moved around her, and opening her enhanced senses to the world. When she finished, she wiped the sweat from her face and headed inside.

She loved this time, the silent house, and that she alone was awake in the village where she'd grown up, partaking in a familiar lifestyle she didn't get to live on most days. She used a combination of magic and elbow grease to clean the kitchen until it was sparkling, then did the same with the other rooms on the house's first floor. On some mornings, she set herself to more active tasks like gathering wood, tending to the garden, or doing whatever the community might need. Today, she wanted the feeling of "home" that working in the house provided.

Unlike some coven members, she didn't have a particular skill that lent itself to certain tasks. Those who were good with fabrics made clothes. Those skilled with wood crafted tools and decorations. Her most valuable skill was a willingness to take on hard work, much like her older sister. Their mother was accomplished at herb lore and supplied the coven with spices and potions. Aisling would be a technomancer before long, and those skills would find a way to serve the community as well.

What Cait had to give, she gave. By the time her family awoke, the house was clean, and breakfast was ready. She had made buckwheat pancakes and oatmeal with fruit, honey, and maple syrup to go along with them. A pot of coffee rested on the table beside another, filled with tea. Brianna looked at her sleepily as she took her seat. "Man, I wish I had your talent for resting. Must be what comes from being a fundamentally lazy person."

Cait snorted a laugh. "Yeah, that's what it is. Sure. Did you notice the breakfast?"

"Eh. Mom does that every day."

Her mother appeared and smacked Brianna on the back of the head. "Are you suggesting that I, too, am lazy?"

Aisling slid into her seat and grabbed the coffee. "She was. I'm sure of it. You should ground her."

They laughed together, then Cait shared the first part of her conversation with the fox. After her revelation that challenging times awaited the coven, Moira shook her head. "Well, that certainly puts the pressure on."

Brianna said, "You know you're the best choice."

"You might be biased."

Cait replied, "Maybe, but that doesn't mean she's

wrong. If strength, wisdom, and compassion are needed, that's your description. So, you'll need to be sure that you are chosen."

Aisling corrected, "That *we* are chosen. "

"Right. That we are chosen."

Moira scowled as she poured syrup onto her pancakes. "Politics. All is politics. This is why your father spends so much time away."

Brianna flashed a grin at Cait, then replied, "Nah. He just doesn't like you."

The jibe earned her a strawberry to the face, thrown by their mother, and the food fight was on. With the mood changed, Cait didn't feel right mentioning the other part of what the fox had told her, about the danger to her personally, so she pushed it to the back of her mind. *Plenty of time to worry about that after light turns to dark.*

The day passed in a happy blur, filled with additional chores, more training, and circulating among the other coven members as they appeared outside, renewing acquaintances and making connections. She would have done it anyway and did so whenever time allowed, but now it took on extra importance. *Politics. Always politics.*

As twilight arrived, she told her family she was headed back up to the mountain and would return to Boston from there. Her mother asked, "You'll be here in a week, though, for the meeting, correct?"

Cait nodded. "Of course. Count on it." She returned to her room and pulled out a set of clothes she hadn't worn in some time. Leather pants again, but thicker than the others, with reinforced panels over shins, thighs, and hamstrings, plus the same along the outside of her upper legs, sufficient to blunt an impact or snarl up a blade. She pulled on a t-shirt, then over it a top that matched the trousers with reinforced pieces in similar locations and metal reinforcements to empower elbow strikes, matching those on the pants that covered her knees.

She slipped on her hiking boots again, those being the most comfortable and durable she owned. Next, she pulled two packs from her wardrobe. One was empty, and she shoved what she thought of as her Columbus clothes—now Boston clothes—into it. The other was full of items she might need depending on what she faced ahead. She wouldn't go in expecting a fight, but neither would she be unprepared for one if it arrived.

Finally, she grabbed a walking stick that stood in a corner, a shillelagh her teacher had gifted her some years before. It was stout, finely balanced, and perfect for her height and strength. She judged she was ready, crossed the packs' straps over her chest to hang at either side of her lower back, and headed out.

She repeated her walk from the night before. This time, as she climbed toward the pinnacle of the mountain, a new set of symbols appeared to guide her away from the path she was familiar with. They led her over rocky scrambles and uncertain ground, and once she had to climb a twenty-foot vertical section, but none of it was overwhelmingly daunting. At the end of the way, she discovered a cave entrance into the mountain, a wide crack that looked natural rather than carved.

She scowled at it. "I'm not a big fan of caves, fox spirit. Thing. Dude." Calling upon her magic, she rotated her right hand and summoned a ball of lightning contained in force, then levitated it ahead of her into the cleft. The passage went into the mountain a few feet, then angled away. "Of course, being able to see what I'm getting myself into would be way too easy."

She stepped inside, feeling the press of the walls and ceiling as they loomed around her. Her enhanced senses detected magic ahead, which, given the circumstances, wasn't unexpected. She also felt an inkling of danger, of something that was not as it should be. She stopped, reached into the bag behind her, and pulled out three items. She buckled the belt around her waist, pushing it down to settle its not insignificant weight in place. It held potions, emergency rations and water, and other survival tools.

Her father had equipped it for her, explaining that one couldn't always rely on magic and especially not depend on the ability to simply portal out of dangerous situations. It had sounded like a lesson learned from personal experience at the time, so she hadn't argued. The items within had proved useful on any number of occasions, even though she'd never been in a situation where something blocked her ability to portal to safety. *And hopefully never will be.*

Next was a pair of wrist sheaths, which held daggers almost as long as her forearms. The right one strapped so the blade was under her arm, and the left so it was on top, permitting her to draw them simultaneously. The blades were crafted from an amalgam of metals found on Oriceran and had been a gift from her father, presumably discovered on an expedition to the other planet. Etchings covered half of each blade, front and back, but no one had ever been able to tell her what they meant.

Her bracelet magically expanded as she pushed it up her arm to rest near her elbow, where it wouldn't damage her draw. If she'd used the weapons more often, she probably would have figured out a different way to use her wand, maybe inserting it into the sheath itself or crafting rings instead. So far, it hadn't been enough of an issue to warrant addressing.

She rounded what turned out to be a final corner and stepped out into a comparatively open space. The cavern was probably twenty feet wide and half that long, and the ceiling above arched several stories high. Purple crystals glittered across it as if she had entered the inside of a geode, and the magical power washing off them almost took her breath away.

A roar brought her attention back to the cave's center, where a bear reacted to her intrusion in less than welcoming tones. The beast was at least two and a half times her height and probably four times her weight. It stood on its rear paws, giant forepaws with wicked curved claws in the air, and locked its eyes on hers. It wavered in her vision, and she realized it wasn't an ordinary bear, but some sort of spirit made flesh.

"Well, hell," she said in the instant before the bear snarled and stalked toward her.

CHAPTER TWELVE

Cait tossed her shillelagh from hand to hand as the bear approached, warming up her muscles. Each step closer made her more cognizant of the size disparity. She muttered, "This better be worth it, fox, whatever you've gotten me into." She pictured the spectral fox laughing at her, thinking it a fine joke to send her against some sort of spirit bear.

It curved around to her left, very clearly stalking her. "All right, beastie. At least we know we're both here for the same thing." It rushed at her, and she dove to the side to avoid a swipe of its paw. Its speed was impressive for something so large, and she compensated by pushing magic into her muscles to make herself faster and stronger. *Not that even my enhanced strength comes near being equal to the bear's.*

When it charged again, she feinted left, went right, and whipped her club down at its leg as it passed. She put a lot of energy behind the blow, and her surprise was complete when it failed to connect. Off-balance, she turned the stumble into a spin and dashed away to gain some distance, her mind busy babbling unbelieving, incoherent curses.

When she'd reached a safe distance with no sound of pursuit, she spun back. The bear was looking at her with its head tilted. *Is that thing smiling?* "Are you mocking me, you four-legged furball?" Its mouth opened, and its tongue lolled out the side. "Let me guess, that's your version of a laugh."

Cait shifted her shillelagh to her left hand and reached for her power, throwing a burst of force magic. It struck the bear's chest but landed without any impact. She narrowed her eyes at something she thought she'd seen and threw another bolt, slightly more powerful, into the same spot. The bear weathered the blow without reacting, but inwardly, Cait's spirits lifted. *So that's your game, huh?*

She charged, and the bear rushed to meet her. Before making her swing, she shot a blast of force magic at the thing's leg. Where it hit, the bear became somehow more solid, more visible, shifting from semi-transparent to fully translucent. She swung at it with her club, again putting all her strength behind the blow in a fit of optimism, and this time, it connected. The bear snarled as it swiped a paw at her, retreated, and scrabbled to orient itself for another pass. She said, "I've got your number, fuzz face. You sure you don't want to give this up?"

His charge suggested he didn't. This time, he leapt over her force blast and pivoted to face her as he landed, digging his back claws into the stone floor. His front paw whipped out, and she summoned a force shield between them. It kept the sharp nails from penetrating but only absorbed some of the blow's power. She was knocked flying and slammed down hard, skidding across the uneven, rocky surface.

Her thick leather protected her from injuries more dire than bruises, and she turned the tumble into a roll, which became a leap to her feet. When the bear attacked again, she summoned a wall of force into its path. It skidded to a stop before impact, and she dispelled the barrier and blasted the creature in the chest with force magic. She dashed in on magically augmented legs, slammed the head of her club into its chest, then ducked under the dual swings it made in response. It was a viable strategy but a dangerous one. One mistake, and she would wind up flying again, at best. *Or skewered, at worst.*

They made several more passes. Cait struck it with magic and her shillelagh, and the bear swung and occasionally connected with her defenses. She shifted her magic from attack to protection in a repeated pattern and said a quiet prayer to the universe that her club would hold up. *It's designed to fight people, not giant spirit bears.*

The realization that the bear was becoming more solid throughout the fight dawned on her slowly. *I wonder.* She altered her strategy, focusing on hitting areas she hadn't yet struck. The bear grew angry as she did so, reassuring her that she was on the right track.

Finally, when only a part of its back she hadn't been able to reach was left unscathed, she dashed forward and launched herself into the air on a burst of force magic. She flew directly over the thing's head, slammed more force into its back, and brought her club crashing down. The bear bucked underneath her, knocking her sideways, and she slammed into the cavern wall after hurtling at least a dozen feet. She managed to protect her head from the impact, but the rest of her felt it keenly, and she slumped to the floor, dazed.

Had the bear still been trying to kill her, her road would have ended there, under the mountain. Instead, it rose on all fours again and gave her that mysterious smile. It bowed, bending at its shoulders, then faded from view, first going transparent before disappearing entirely.

Cait groaned and forced herself up, knowing that to remain on the floor would only make the eventual need to rise all that much more difficult. The fox walked into the area from the passageway, fully present rather than ghostly. It sat and awarded her a nod, presumably of approval.

She asked, "Did I do what you wanted me to do?"

The fox replied, "You've defeated the first of guardians three. Do not delay, for you must conquer all before the sun rises." It turned without waiting for an answer and walked through the passage that led from the room's far side.

Cait groaned and called after him, "You're a jerk, you know? The whole mysterious messenger thing is totally overdone." Her body and mind were depleted, having exhausted a lot of her physical and magical power against the bear. She considered drinking her energy potion but remembered where she was.

Slowly, she lowered herself to her knees, let her weight settle back on her heels, and rested her hands gently on her thighs. She programmed her brain to give her a wake-up call, then let her thoughts fall inward. After nine minutes—three threes—she rose refreshed.

She brushed off the leather at her shins and murmured, "Not fully rested, but much better. Thanks, Patrick." The mountain didn't reply. A brisk stride took her along the path from the room the fox had used. This passage was different from the one she'd been in, toolwork clear on the hewn surfaces around her. Crystals were embedded in a straight line on either side at shoulder height, granting light and caressing her with their magic.

Symbols ran along each wall, ones she had never seen before. She whispered a spell to help her interpret the carvings and gained a vague understanding that they were all about moments of change—bridges over chasms, crossroads where multiple paths met, flying high, swimming deep. They captured her full attention as she tried to divine their meanings, and she reached the next opening without any recollection of the path she'd taken to get there. *Great job, Cait.*

Unlike the rocky chamber where she'd encountered the bear, this area seemed like an indoor forest, lit from above by a cluster of purple crystals that stood in for the sun. A brook ran through the center, bisecting the room horizontally, and trees lined most of the areas to her left and right. A worn dirt path traveled to the brook, across it, and toward the other exit. No obvious danger presented itself. She put her hands on her hips, shook her head, and announced, "No way am I stupid enough to think this is safe."

She shifted the shillelagh to her left hand and called up a tight force shield around her, less than an inch away from her skin. It moved as she did, and she would be able to maintain it if she had to evade. As she neared the center, a rustle came from her right, and she slowed her steps.

One of the trees turned out not to be a tree. *Or, well, not only a tree.* Its trunk split into legs and what had seemed to be branches turned out to be arms with sharp thorns for fingers. A face appeared in the bark, and its eyes opened. The creature was at least twelve feet tall, and the smaller branches and leaves at its top looked like a crown.

Cait said, "Hi there, nice tree person. I don't want any trouble."

Its battle cry sounded like the snapping of wood. It slashed both branchy arms forward, and a wave of projectiles flew at her. She summoned an angled shield and crouched behind it without abandoning the protection around her body. Her mental voice supplied, "More like cowering than crouching, if you ask me."

No one did. Shut up. Inner Cait was a total wench on her best days. When the small objects struck the shield, they exploded, forcing her to pour more power into the defense. When the barrage stopped, she straightened and called, "Did you throw acorns at me? Seriously? Exploding acorns?"

She hurled a ball of fire at it, realizing only afterward what a stupid idea that was, given the general flammability of the room's contents. It struck the tree and vanished, not singeing even a leaf. She took a few steps toward it and tried frost magic, which also failed to do any harm. Lightning next, then force, but nothing worked.

Shadow was always an option, but one her coven rejected categorically. Some thought it would be acceptable to use it in a case where it could make a difference between life and death. Others believed death would be preferable to such a compromise, viewing shadow as tainted with evil. She didn't get into the metaphysics of it all, merely chose not to use it.

"Guess we do this the old-fashioned way." She ran forward and swung the shillelagh at it, immediately falling into a roll afterward to avoid the swipe from its talons. It felt like hitting the mountain itself, and her hand immediately ached from the blow. She dashed out of range, thankful that at least the animated tree moved slowly.

It opened its mouth and vomited a thick goo onto the surface near her. A bit slopped onto her foot and slowed her as it tried to stick her to the ground. "Sap? Gross." Cait slid the shillelagh into the leather loop on one of her backpack straps and drew her knives in a smooth movement. She scraped one against the stuff, and the sap recoiled in response, dropping from her boot to the dirt. She looked up at the tree with a grin. "Oh, so you don't like metal, huh?"

She ran at her wooden foe again, not sure exactly how the vulnerability to her knives would prove out. *I'll probably be chopping at this thing for the next millennium.* It emitted a low thrumming noise, deep and alarming, and a wave of buzzing dots flew out of the trees. She coated herself with force magic again, doubling her shield, and ignored the attack. The wasps slammed into her, seemingly crazed, stingers stabbing in repeatedly. Her shield blocked them from penetrating, although each impact was a tiny mote of pain that quickly made her whole body feel like she was being rubbed down with coarse sandpaper.

The flow of flying creatures didn't stop, but she

continued to ignore it as she dove out of the way of another blast of sap. She'd angled the evasion to put her behind the tree and moved with it as it tried to rotate to get at her, its actions too slow to be a problem. She chopped at a single spot with her blades, pausing all too often to push wasps away from her eyes so she could see, and bark chipped off satisfyingly.

She threaded energy into her arms to continue the attack as she grew tired, finally breaking through the outer protection and revealing pure wood inside. When her metal touched its inner surface, the tree shivered, its leaves fell, and it froze in place, motionless.

She sprinted for the crevice at the far end of the room, stopping inside. When she crossed the threshold into the passage, the tree shivered again. Its bark extended to cover the wound she'd created, and it turned to face her. The newly reappeared leaves on its branches rustled as it waved, and the creature moved back to its hidden position among the trees. She shook her head. "Sure. Wood is immune to wood or something. And magic, I guess. I'll file that one away in my mental notebook of useless facts."

She turned to see the fox sitting primly in the corridor. He said, "You're doing well. One to go. But the world spins while you delay, Caitriona, daughter of Moira, bringing sunrise and failure with it."

CHAPTER THIRTEEN

As Cait walked through the passage toward whatever new challenge lay ahead, muttering threats at the fox, who had vanished again, something happened. It felt, for a moment, like the world around her lurched slightly before realigning itself. She laughed at the thought of an old movie and wondered if she'd see a black cat walking in front of her. *Glitch in the matrix. Something's changed.*

The heat from the next chamber reached her from around the corner. She raised one arm to guard her eyes against it as she made the turn, expecting fire even though she couldn't see it. Instead, she found a room of glassy black stone with a bright creature slithering in random patterns upon it. She squinted against the haze shimmering in the air and identified it as a giant snake, to all appearances composed of lava.

She growled, "You've got to be kidding me," and sheathed her knives, exchanging them for her shillelagh. She figured that she would want to keep the monstrosity as far away as possible, no matter what.

Cait approached it slowly, and it hissed as it spotted her, expelling steam from its mouth along with a flicker of a molten tongue. It didn't move to the attack, thankfully, perhaps unable to fit into the passageway or not permitted to do so by the rules of whatever game the fox had sent her to play. She built her magic to increase the potency of her next spell, corralling it when it wanted to escape her control.

When she let it loose, a continuous stream of frost jetted from her open hand, impacting the creature where its body met the floor. Where her cold magic hit, the snake turned to stone. The lava portion continued moving while the small gray boulder she'd created stayed in place.

She frowned at the result. "No way it's that easy." Lacking any better idea, she repeated the process several times from the mouth of the passage, blasting the lava snake until it was mostly converted to stone. She stepped into the room when only a small portion remained, still slithering aimlessly around the middle. It charged her when she crossed the threshold, but she intercepted the last molten remnant with a final burst of magic. It turned to stone, and she shrugged. "Okay, fox. Was that it?"

With a rumble that shook the entire room, the boulders she'd created started to move. They rolled into a line, then somehow joined enough that the whole front portion rose, the lava snake now turned into some kind of boulder cobra. It slithered toward her, and its chest, for lack of a better word, slammed down at her.

She dove out of the way and came up running, headed for the opposite opening. A glimmer of magic warned her that she wouldn't be able to pass through. She spun to face the new creature she'd inadvertently produced, hopping over the tail that swished at her legs.

She muttered, "Well, I guess a snake made of rocks is preferable to one made of lava. At least it can't burn me." She tried throwing frost magic at it again, but this time it had no impact. As it chased her, she sidestepped, cut, and rolled to avoid its attacks while trying each of her other magics against it.

Fire was useless, and lightning scored the surface but didn't slow or stop it. She hit it with a burst of force, and though it dodged, the blast caught it at the junction of two boulders in its tail. They separated, and the one that rolled away split and fell into black shards that matched the other stone in the room.

"Okay, I think I get it." She fired additional blasts of force magic, but unfortunately, she wasn't the only one in the battle who learned. The snake was quick to evade her attacks, rolling out of the way with more speed than she had credited it.

After a minute of fruitless exchanges, the serpent seemed as frustrated by the impasse as she was. It would dart forward, she would counter with force magic, and it would evade. She'd attack, and it would dodge. Then the process repeated itself.

Cait growled, "Guess this will need to be a little more up close and personal." She covered herself in force magic, reinforced her shillelagh with more of it, and pushed the rest of her available magic pool into her muscles for speed.

She raced at the snake, dove and rolled sideways as it tried to fall on her again, and came up running at its back. Her weapon struck the seam where the tail met the body, and a three-boulder section fell away. It didn't transform into a different material as the last had but instead attacked her separately.

She yelped and ran faster, shouting, "Not fair." *I'm so glad no one is here to see this comedy of stupidity.* The serpent didn't care about the lack of fairness. She turned her attention to chopping off the last boulder in line with the main body or the detached tail, whichever was closer when she found an opportunity to attack.

After several more passes, she'd reduced the tail to nothing and was face-to-face with the large snake. It swayed in front of her, again dodging her force blasts as she kept it at a distance so she could shift from blind instinct to actual thought.

It had come close to catching her several times, and she was running out of energy. *Well, I can take care of one of those problems easily enough.* While she continued to throw magic at the creature, she dropped her club and used that hand to grab a potion and pop the top. She drank the bright blue liquid, and magical energy surged through her. As her telekinesis brought her club back to smack into her empty hand, she got an idea.

Cait reached out with her magic to a shard of the sharp rock that littered the cavern, grabbed it, and pulled it toward her. Halfway along its path, she redirected it, sending it slicing through the join between the rearmost boulder and the snake's body. Both boulders it touched transformed into like material, and the serpent grew smaller. She laughed and broke off a second fragment of the room's stone, hurling it forward to carve another section off the snake. A few moments later, the fight was over.

The fox appeared in the passage ahead. "Congratulations. You may continue onward, for you have succeeded." It padded beside her as she complied. She had questions but felt that asking them would be somehow inappropriate. A surprisingly short time later, they walked out of the corridor into twilight.

Cait said, "What the hell?" A glance down to her right revealed that the fox she'd been about to question had vanished. She looked up at the stars and realized they weren't the ones she expected. "I'm on Oriceran. How did that happen?" Her steps carried her forward into a clearing. Her senses screamed danger, and she fell into a defensive crouch, peering around her for its source. When a giant dragon landed beside her, she yelped in surprise, having not included "up" in her assessment.

The imposing creature didn't attack but simply asked in a deep voice, "What are you doing, witchling?"

She rose from her crouch and shoved her shillelagh back in its holder. "Being an idiot, apparently."

The dragon laughed. "A normal reaction to meeting one of us for the first time. I am Coazzir." It towered above her, easily four times her height, and its scales seemed to shine with an inner light, radiant in blue and red.

"I'm Caitriona, daughter of Moira."

The dragon tilted its head slightly to the side and blinked. Its eyes were deep emerald, with a dark vertical slit. "We do not know you."

Cait shook her head. "No, I think if anyone in my

family had met a dragon before, I'd know it. Should I, like, bow or something?"

In amused tones, the creature replied, "If you wish." She did, and the dragon offered her a slight nod in return. "So, you have completed the ritual."

"I guess? The fox seemed to think so."

"You seem very young."

Cait shrugged. "I suppose, compared to some."

The dragon lowered its snout toward her. "Then I believe it would be appropriate to pair you with another like yourself."

Cait's brain hiccupped. "Pair me?"

Her words got lost in the dragon's roar. As the sound echoed around the clearing, five smaller dragons in different colors and sizes appeared. They flew circles around the clearing, and after the third go-round, one of them soared in toward her, performing a barrel roll as it approached. Having never experienced a horse-sized flying creature hurtling at her before, Cait ducked and congratulated herself for not dropping to the ground.

He landed in front of her, shrank quickly to the size of a small dog, then jumped up into her arms. She caught him reflexively since her brain was entirely offline from surprise. Inside her mind, she heard a satisfied, *"Mine."* His scales were rainbow-colored, pulsing as if they weren't sure what color they wanted to be. Examining them closer, she saw that their shape was exactly like Coazzir's, only smaller, like leaves spreading from the base then coming together at the tip.

She scratched his head instinctively, and he made a contented noise. Looking up at the larger dragon, Cait asked, "What's going on? Did something happen to me, and now I'm in heaven where everyone gets a dragon friend?"

Another chuckle emanated from Coazzir. "You are very much alive, witchling. You and he will share your lives, protecting one another henceforth. Through the ritual, you have proven yourself worthy of this partnership. His name is Azasainia."

Cait peered down at him. "Aza? I'm Cait." He responded with a snore. She looked up at the immense dragon. "Is he always like this?"

A laugh accompanied what was unmistakably a smile, albeit a *very* toothy one. "No. Usually, he's much more troublesome."

Cait sighed. "Of course he is."

CHAPTER FOURTEEN

After offering her goodbyes to Coazzir, Cait portaled back to her Boston hotel room, which completely failed to rouse the puppy-sized dragon in her arms. The time zone changes between her village in Ireland, Oriceran, and Boston left her no time for anything but a quick shower, fast dressing, and hitting the exit at a run to the nearest Starbucks. Aza was comfortably curled in a ball, the tip of his tail touching his nose, fully asleep on her bed as she closed the door and dropped the "Do Not Disturb" sign onto the handle.

She made it to the office only five minutes late, waved at Sabrina, and crossed to her desk. The office was well lit, almost making up for its lack of windows. The off-white tile floor showed patterns between the desks and more wear toward the chief's office on the back left. The Marshals' desks each held down a section of the space, and they probably could have easily fit double the amount.

She had only just logged in and checked her messages

when Garrett's smile appeared above her displays. "Hey, Cait. Busy weekend?"

She tucked a stray piece of hair that had fallen onto her face behind her ear. "Is it obvious?"

He laughed. "If you hadn't said you were visiting your family, I would've figured you'd been on a forty-eight-hour bender. You've got that tired but wild, energized look about you."

"You know that's a contradiction, right?"

He shrugged. "And yet, I see it; I say it."

"I'm sure those around you love you for that."

He laughed and turned toward the door, waving in a "come along" gesture. "Less than you'd think. Come on. We're going to visit the dead."

They descended to the subway station in the building's basement and stepped onto the first train to pull up. They both remained standing, instincts guiding them to a position at one end of the car where they could watch the other passengers. She said, "So, the morgue?"

"You pierced my clever wordsmithing. You should consider going into law enforcement."

"I'm guessing people don't call you clever that often, do they?"

He laughed. "Again, less than you'd think."

She leaned closer to him and asked quietly, "Do we have new information?"

He offered a noncommittal shrug. "I've got an in with one of the folks who works there. She suggested we should visit."

At the next stop, the car grew more crowded, and they shifted their talk from professional to personal. As they moved through subterranean Boston, she learned that Garrett had a wife and two kids, both sons. He volunteered as a Scout leader almost every weekend, and the family spent time each week taking care of elderly parishioners in their church.

Cait came away from the conversation even more convinced that her new place of employment would be a good home for her. They reached their stop, then walked a couple of blocks through the crisp sunshine to reach the morgue. It was in a nondescript building, with offices on the second and third floors and the more grisly functional areas on the first floor and basement.

Garrett knew where he was going and after they'd signed in, led her directly down a hallway to an unmarked door. She braced herself for what might lie beyond it, expecting metal tables and too-still bodies. Instead, it opened onto a small office with two desks set up as mirror images of one another.

A woman sat at one of them, and she rose at their arrival. Garrett said, "Priscilla, nice to see you. This is Keane."

Cait extended her hand. "Call me Cait."

The other woman replied, "Good to meet you." She turned her attention to Garrett. "I've got something interesting for you."

He yawned, covering it with a belated hand. "Don't make me wait. The excitement is killing me. "

"I can't imagine what that saint you married sees in you."

He grinned. "Play your cards right, and maybe she'll invite you to find out."

Priscilla rolled her eyes. "Eww." She sat again and hit a button on the keyboard, summoning an image to her monitors. "Take a look at this."

Cait leaned forward and frowned at the picture. It showed deliberate markings of some kind, obviously carved into flesh. She asked, "From the judge?"

"Yep."

"While he was still alive?"

The other woman's face didn't change. "Yep." *Guessing she sees things a lot worse than this every day in a big city like this.*

Garrett had his hands on the desk, leaning over to look at the pictures more closely. "That's so weird. Anyone recognize them?"

Priscilla shook her head, and Cait said, "Not I. Can you send these over to me?" The other woman's fingers worked on the keyboard, and the images appeared on Cait's phone. "Thanks."

Their host asked, "Any theories?"

She shrugged. "Someone didn't like him much if they were cutting him in addition to the other stuff they did."

Priscilla laughed without amusement. "Safe bet."

They said their goodbyes, and when they got outside, Garrett said, "You don't think those are a language, right?"

"No. But we should have Sabrina check into it, anyway."

"I'm all over that. Already sent them to her." He paused for a moment, then came to a decision. "Let's swing by the police station that caught the case."

Cait looked doubtfully at him. "You think the detectives are going to share information?"

He shrugged. "Probably not. But no stone left unturned is what we do, right?"

The station aligned much more closely with her expectations than the morgue had. The bottom floor was all intake and processing. The real action happened on the second level, where detectives and investigators sat scattered among cubicles in a giant room. Garrett wandered through, exchanging greetings with several of them before finding who he was looking for at the coffee maker.

The woman was short and looked like life had aged her before her time, etching lines into her skin under dark hair that showed some gray at the roots. A slight frown that was probably a permanent fixture had been on her lips as they'd approached. She carried a few extra pounds, but they looked good on her, and her suit and blouse fit well. "Garrett. How lovely to see you *here*." The tone of her voice suggested suspicion.

He replied, "Heard you were working the judge case."

"Heard you were, too." The woman dumped three packets of sugar into her paper cup of coffee and swirled it to mix them.

"True that. Didn't see you at the scene."

She scowled. "My partner got there first, so I got stuck doing neighbor checks."

He laughed. "Next time, you'll drive faster."

The other woman sipped her drink. "Right?" She looked at Cait. "Hi. He's rude, and I'm Veronica Westra."

"Cait Keane."

Garrett asked, "What do you know?"

The detective stared down at her coffee as she swirled it and sighed. "Not a damn thing. I presume you've seen the cuts?"

Cait replied, "Yeah."

"Current thinking is they might have something to do with the Dragons. Or to be more specific, that's what the organized crime taskforce believes."

Garrett asked, "And you?"

She took another sip of her coffee, scowled, and threw the cup into a nearby garbage can. "I think they're under the mistaken impression that the symbols are Chinese characters. They must be looking for a secret language, though, since a two-minute computer search confirmed they don't match any known alphabet." She looked around once. "Coffee sucks. Want to step out with me to get a decent cup?"

When they were out on the street, Veronica said, "This feels like it's going to be a hot one. Just instinct telling me that, but I'm right more often than not. I'm up for information-sharing if you are but under the table. The organized crime detectives are pretty territorial, and I don't need to draw any attitude from them."

Garrett nodded. "For sure." Cait agreed.

The conversation paused while they stepped into a coffee shop and ordered drinks, then resumed once they were back on the street. The detective said, "Rumor has it that the judge wasn't necessarily as squeaky clean as he pretended to be."

Garrett frowned. "Involved with the Roses or Dragons, you think?"

She nodded. "One or the other. That's what we hear, anyway. You might want to go through his notes, that kind of stuff."

Cait's partner's expression was dark as he replied, "Damn."

Veronica acknowledged, "I know. Sucks to have to investigate one of your own. Remember, if you find anything, you owe me." The detective wandered off with a wave, headed back toward the police building.

Garrett said, "Suddenly, I doubt this case will be the fun-filled career-making joyride I thought it would be."

Cait replied, "Right there with you, partner. Time to revisit the crime scene and give it a serious look with more suspicious eyes."

CHAPTER FIFTEEN

The house looked notably different in the daytime. No crime scene tape, no ambulances and police cars hovering nearby, no neighbors standing around watching the hullabaloo and sharing guesses about what was going on. She rang the doorbell, and a good-looking woman in her fifties with perfectly done brown hair and flawless makeup opened the door. Cait asked, "Mrs. Elizabeth Meyer?"

The judge's wife nodded. "Yes?" Her outfit looked as if she was ready for a day at the spa, loose and comfortable yet elegant, pants and a sweater in off-white.

"Deputy Marshals Keane and Bradley, ma'am. Could we talk to you for a moment?"

The woman sighed and stepped away from the door, leaving it open. "Of course." She led them into the well-appointed living room and gestured for them to take seats on the couch. She lowered herself carefully into a nearby chair with the fragility Cait had seen in the bereaved before.

"What can I do for you?" Her voice cracked slightly. "This is all so awful. I still can't believe he's gone. Every noise I hear, I expect it to be him coming home like everything is okay." She shook her head with sadness on her face.

Garrett asked in a surprisingly soft tone, "Our records say you were out of town the night of the incident?"

Mrs. Meyer sniffed, then nodded. "Yes. At the board meeting for the charity I work for. In Chicago. Of course, I had to come back early, as soon as I heard."

She seemed to Cait as if she was still processing the shock of her husband's death. "We're trying to figure out a motive for the attack. Do you have any ideas?"

The other woman shrugged. "Someone he prosecuted, most likely." Cait exchanged glances with her partner, and he gave a slight nod, indicating that he'd noticed the change in Mrs. Meyer's demeanor. *So, what is it you're worried about us discovering?*

Garrett asked, "Any other possible reason you can think of? Anything different of late or out of the ordinary?"

She leaned back, shaking her head. Her body language indicated resistance to the questions. "No. Not at all."

Cait, realizing the woman had closed down as a source, asked, "May we look around? See if there's something we missed?"

The wife sighed, sounding exasperated. "We've had people all over the place. Sure, why the hell not?" She lifted a hand and said in a more reserved tone, "I'm sorry. This is all a bit much."

Cait rose. "We understand, Mrs. Meyer. We'll be out of your hair as quickly as we can."

Their first stop was the upstairs bedroom, where someone had removed the entire bed, leaving a space on the floor. She whispered the words to activate her magic senses but detected no other power in the room. She muttered, "That would've been too easy."

Garrett was systematically opening drawers and peering inside. "What?"

"Nothing magic in the room."

"Ah. Guess we'll have to do it the old-fashioned way rather than using your woo-woo powers."

She laughed. "Woo-woo. Really? I'm coming around to wondering what your wife sees in you as well." He opened his mouth, and she interrupted, "Don't say anything. Shh. I'm working." Focusing her will, she murmured, "Current and wave, water and air; motion reveal, motion declare. Use the breeze to show what's there." A gentle waft of air passed slowly through the room from left to right. It rippled in her vision as it caused previously unseen dust to move, showing patterns of what was well-used and what wasn't. Unfortunately, nothing seemed out of the ordinary.

She repeated the spells in the attached bathroom, again finding no evidence of anything unexpected. His office held more dust than the bedroom had, but none of the heavy use areas showed anything suspicious. She gestured at his computer. "I presume we're already addressing that?"

Garrett nodded. "Cloned hard drive. We've got a copy and so does the PD. I can't imagine any amateurs hiding secrets electronically in this day and age, though."

Cait frowned at the office, surly over its lack of cooperation. "Agreed. Is there a game room or something? Man cave?"

He laughed. "Nope. Only their kid's room and a downstairs family room, plus kitchen and garage."

"Let's try the garage first." That space was considerably dustier, but when she cast her spell, an unexpected path appeared. It led to the bottom part of a tool bench that looked like a riser to put the tools in better reach. She knelt and ran her fingertips over it and around the sides, eventually discovering a slight depression. When she put her finger in it and lifted, the case slid open. "Well, what do we have here?"

Garrett knelt beside her. "Looks like a safe to me. Are you sure you're a marshal?" It was heavy metal, with a small touchscreen and a numerical keypad.

She retorted, "I guess you've never heard of a rhetorical question, huh? Biometrics and code. Reasonably secure."

He offered a wry smile. "Not against us." He reached into his inner pocket, pulled out a device, and set it next to the keypad. It stuck there, presumably magnetically. "Codebreaker," he explained. "Wireless access to the electronics inside."

She nodded at the screen. "And for that?"

"Some time ago, the morgue updated its protocols. Now, in addition to all the pictures, they also have retinal scans, fingerprints, and handprints. Even footprints."

"Have you had a reason to need a footprint?"

Garrett fiddled with his phone. "No. I figure that's in there for completeness. Or because someone in the police department has a particular interest in feet." He looked up quickly to see her response, and she rolled her eyes at him. He laughed. "Okay, here we go."

A button push switched on the codebreaker, and while

it did its work, he held his phone up to the biometric pad. When the device found the correct number, the pad activated, scanning the phone. The lock made a loud *thunk* as it released.

Cait turned the handle, opened it, and discovered bundles of cash—not the new ones you'd get from a bank, but bills that had been in use. The safe was full of them, and they were mostly hundreds. "Wow."

Garrett sighed. "Moments like this test one's character. Both my kids are going to need braces, eventually. One stack could probably pay for them and send us on vacation."

She grabbed a book that rested on top of the cash, pulling it out to open it. "Yeah, that's how you wind up on the wrong side of the bars, my friend."

"There should be a finder's fee. Merit bonus. Incentive. Something."

She frowned down at the book and held it out to him. "Lots of numbers." The left column increased from top to bottom on each page, but not in any linear pattern, except that it started in single digits, moved to double, then triple. Beside it, the center column was alphanumeric and varied in the number of characters from one entry to the next. The third column was almost certainly money, some of the records in parentheses. "Clearly a ledger."

Garrett shrugged. "Yeah. My first guess is payoffs."

"Then why the negatives? If that's what the parentheses are, that is."

"Cash on hand versus deposits?"

She sighed and closed the ledger. "Or maybe he was a middle person for someone else. The wife might know, but

I doubt she's going to talk. We could spend the rest of the day guessing and still not get it right."

He stood with a groan. "You're right. But we've got an expert who can take a run at figuring it out. Unfortunately, she's off the clock until tomorrow." Cait looked down at her watch and was surprised to see that it was after five. "Want to grab a drink at the club?"

She laughed because the team's nickname for The Shillelagh was obvious and perfect. "Sure."

He put the book back inside and called in an evidence team to collect it and the ledger. When they arrived to take custody of the materials, Garret led her out toward the car. "They make a mean steak."

Cait shook her head. "I'm in a seafood town after living in Ohio, for heaven's sake. I've had enough cow to last me at least a few years."

As they reached the sedan, Garrett replied, "Well then, fresh-caught lobster, it is."

She grinned at him across the roof. "Now you're talking."

CHAPTER SIXTEEN

After a good meal and engaging conversation with Garrett and Clement, who arrived a little later, Cait stopped at a small grocery store near her hotel. She had no idea what dragons ate but figured it would be important to find out. *Hopefully, he hasn't gone mad from hunger and ripped the place apart, or worse.* Aza had been on her mind the whole day, guilt over leaving him alone coloring every experience. *It's possible I'm not cut out to be a pet owner. Er, life partner. Whatever.*

When she tentatively opened the door to her hotel room, braced for the worst, she found the dragon lying on his back on her bed. The cover was tangled and mussed beneath him, and he had all four paws in the air. He rolled over at her entrance and climbed to his feet, then extended one front leg and stretched like a cat, the second joining it shortly thereafter. He completed the stretch with his back legs, leaning forward, and hopped down while visibly sniffing.

The dragon was beautiful, his scales shining as if they

were metallic, multicolored, and with no obvious pattern, but nonetheless striking and unearthly. In her mind, he said, *"What have you brought?"* His voice was eager, warm, and playful.

She grabbed the comforter from the bed and spread it on the floor, then sat on a corner and patted the spot beside her. He hopped over to it and sat, front paws straight, back paws collapsed in a dog-like pose.

She laid out her finds. "So, on the menu tonight we have fresh-caught raw salmon, fresh-caught cooked salmon, raw beef, cooked beef, cooked pork, and an array of vegetables." Cait tumbled them onto the bedspread and finished, "Oh, and some fruit." She snagged an apple and bit into it, then chewed and swallowed while she offered it to him.

After sniffing it, he shook his head. *"No, thanks."*

"More for me. So, do you prefer your food cooked or raw?"

He replied, "Seared." A tiny puff of smoke came out of each nostril to illustrate the point. Cait laughed and unwrapped the grilled salmon. "Okay, try this." His sharp fangs scraped against her skin as he took it off her palm.

He chomped on it, working it with his side teeth, then swallowed. *"Delicious."*

She grinned. "Of course, you like the most expensive fish. We'll have to try some others, too."

"Expensive?"

"Never mind. Let's see how you feel about this one." She offered him the beef, which had been cooked to medium. *Glad I didn't splurge on Kobe after the salmon experience.*

He ate it, then observed, *"A little undercooked."*

"Noted." Finally, she proffered the pork, but he turned his nose up at it. "Okay. Fish and cow. That's a start." She suspended the other piece of salmon in a box of force and used a magical flame to cook it, then handed it to him.

While he ate, she peeled a banana and chewed it slowly, a sweet treat for the end of the day. She tentatively stroked his scales, which were hard but somehow still flexible. They rippled at her touch, and he made a noise that sounded like comfort. She smiled. "I think we have a lot to learn about each other, my friend."

The enormity of the obligations that now weighed on her was coming into focus. "We'll need to go hunting, I guess. I'll probably have to get a different place to live. With a kitchen and stuff."

"Hunt?" He sounded eager.

"Not the city, of course. No free wildlife here. My people, I mean the witches in my coven, don't believe in eating domesticated animals, only those we hunt for. We keep chickens and such for eggs, but we don't eat them. I think we'll have pretty good access to wild-caught fish here, but meat will be a little more challenging."

"I like hunting."

Cait laughed. "Well then, I can't wait to introduce you to my sisters. We all enjoy it, too." She put the food away and restored the comforter to the bed after shaking it out. "Can you speak?"

He looked at her with partially lowered lids, and she read the expression as a judgment that she'd asked a stupid question. *"Of course."*

"Out loud, I mean?"

He paused, then roared, and she quickly shushed him,

laughing. "Okay, maybe not." *Are you able to hear my thoughts?* No reply came, which was a touch disappointing. "Okay, so not telepathy. I know flying is among your skills, but can you run?"

He hopped off the bed and dashed around the room, achieving decent speed despite the lack of space to move in. "Okay. That's good." She frowned and said, "You know, your scales look different than when I came in."

"That's because they are." He moved to a nearby wall. With a ripple, his scales changed color to match it, making him more difficult to see.

"Oh, that's useful." His mouth shifted into something that she thought resembled a smile. "Fortunately, I don't need to sleep too much, so we'll have time to hang out. I hate that you'll be here alone all day, though. Another reason to find a better living arrangement, I guess, so you'll have room to run. Speaking of running, how about we go for a jog, get to know the neighborhood?"

He moved to the door, clearly in agreement. She changed into running clothes, including a heavy hoodie sweatshirt against the night chill, and led him out into the street. He jogged beside her, maintaining his concealment as they ran. While it was a good precaution, it probably wasn't needed.

They encountered no pedestrians along their path, although an increasing number of cars passed as they neared the docks. She increased her speed, pushing herself. He took to the air, soaring above, looking playful as he dipped and whirled. She spoke low. "Can you hear me?"

His answer came back in her head. *"Yes. I have very good ears."*

She laughed. "Technically, I'm not sure you have ears at all."

"Hearing, then. Don't make me roast you."

She grinned through her panting breaths. "I consider myself totally warned." After an hour, they reached an area of the docks with an all-night fish market, selling fresh-caught fare to the restaurant trade. She secured several kinds, figuring it would be good to see if he had preferences.

They made their way to a slip that wasn't currently home to a boat, and she set the pieces of fish on a slab of force magic, preparing to cook it. He got to it before she did, belching a continuous gout of fire that quickly seared them. Then he grabbed the food, tearing with teeth and claws, almost as if he was enjoying the act of shredding the fish as much as eating it. She laughed. "Those are some pretty fierce weapons you've got there. You'll get to help hunt." He gave her another one of those grins, and she snorted. "Oh yeah, Brianna's gonna love you."

"What's a Brianna?"

"Technically, it's who is Brianna, but your version makes some sense too. She's kind of undefinable." She raced him on the way home, going into sprints that forced him into the air to keep pace, then jogging at a reasonable rate that allowed him to run beside her. He seemed equally comfortable on the ground or in flight, and a vision of them hunting together in the Irish countryside came to her. *One thing's for sure. Almost everything will be at least a little different from here on out.*

She yawned as they hit the door. "Some things will remain the same. I need to shower and get a little sleep before work tomorrow." When she got back to the bed after cleaning up, he was already in it. She climbed under the covers, then shoved him with her back, trying to clear some space. "Did you grow bigger while I was in the shower? Move over, scale head." Finally, they found an arrangement that suited them both, with him lying along the curve of her back. She fell asleep thinking of what kind of backyard she'd need to provide ample room for a dragon to entertain itself. *A really, really big one.*

In the morning, she woke at five instead of four since she'd done her cardio the night before. She flicked on the monitor, called up a yoga routine, and groaned as she stretched tight muscles. She showered again, put on a little makeup, corralled her hair, then looked down at the dragon, who hadn't left the bed. "Guess it's time for me to leave for work. I wish I could take you with me."

He yawned and sat up. *"You can."*

She laughed as she secured her holster to her belt. "I don't think I'll be able to explain a dragon to my colleagues quite yet. They're still adapting to having a magical in their midst. That would probably be a bit too much."

He stood on his front paws and shook his head. *"No, you can. See?"*

She flinched a little as he leapt at her, but he changed in midair, shrinking. He landed on her shoulder and crawled behind her neck, wrapping himself around it. She coughed once from the pressure, then looked in the mirror. He had disguised himself as a choker, a thick band around her neck with only his scales showing. They glittered like jewels.

She touched him, and he felt more like metal than a

living being. "That's hella impressive, Aza, but I can't wear that. It's too, uh, beautiful for work," she said, editing the word "ostentatious" lest she offend the dragon.

He shifted again, lengthening his neck and shrinking, becoming a necklace. Most of his body stayed hidden under her hair, and only his tail and head came around to rest on her chest. It was still more noticeable than she'd like, but an improvement. "Can you dial down the brightness a little?"

His scales rippled, becoming a uniform silver except for his head and tail, which retained some color. Aside from his blinking eyes, she would've guessed him to be inanimate. He asked, *"How's that?"*

She stroked her new living necklace, amazed. "I think that'll work. Unless it sets off the magic detectors. If it does, I suppose I'll have some explaining to do." Her wand made it through, so it was equally possible that he might. "Guess we'll find out. Another day, another adventure."

"But one we're on together." He closed his eyes. *"Which is much, much better."*

CHAPTER SEVENTEEN

Cait made it through the detectors without an issue. They detected active magic rather than the existence of magicals. *Or maybe my being a magical was cleared, and it has a different mode for me. Either way, I should probably figure that out.*

The thought left her brain as she moved through the lobby and stepped into the elevator. She wound up packed in with a bunch of others, and Aza whispered in her mind, *"Who are these people?"*

She remained quiet until she exited the elevator. "Lots of folks work in this building. Others come here for a variety of reasons. Those were some of them."

"One smelled like flowers."

She laughed. The dragon's comments drew mirth from her on a more or less constant basis. "Yeah, I thought her perfume was a bit much, too." Cait's scent of choice was muskier or perhaps spicier. She counted herself lucky that the dragon hadn't commented on it.

She'd expected to get started immediately on tracing

Judge Meyer's money trail, but Garret said they'd need Sabrina for that, and she was busy. So, Cait did more paperwork, spent some time looking at maps of Boston, and more time reviewing the most wanted fugitives in the region. The likelihood that she would ever run into one on the street and recognize him was pretty low, but anything was possible. *As the dragon around my neck goes to show.*

At midmorning, she took a walk around the landscaped grounds of the Moakley, taking the opportunity to answer the questions Aza had been throwing at her all morning. She sensed he was young and interested in learning everything he could. *Well, I guess that kind of makes two of us. One more note of compatibility.*

She stopped for lunch, choosing two lobster rolls minus the butter from a stand that served the courthouse, and surreptitiously shared pieces of them with the dragon. The sight of his little head animating and biting off tiny chunks of the lobster made her laugh from sheer cuteness overload. "Something tells me this will only get more weird, rather than less, as time goes on."

He replied, *"You* are *weird. This is true."*

Her return to the office had her walking a few steps behind Sabrina. The infomancer wore similar attire to what Cait had seen on her before, a flowing black skirt and a hint of cool footwear beneath a vintage-looking blouse and professional blazer. Garrett rose from his desk at her appearance. "Sabrina, are you ready?"

The woman nodded. "Yep. Let's go to the dungeon." Cait's initial reaction, that the infomancer meant the basement, was proved incorrect as she led them to a door at the side of the office. It opened onto a modest room, about twelve feet by twenty, shrouded in darkness. Sabrina said, "Lights," and several small implements glowed, covering the room in hazy illumination tinted with red. The other woman said, "Take the couch. I'll be back in a second. I have to get my battle dress on." She went through another door, closing it behind her.

Cait sat as instructed. Garrett did the same at the far end. It was long enough that she could have laid on it without putting her feet on the arms. She asked, "Battle dress?"

He grinned. "You'll see."

When Sabrina reemerged, her outfit was almost the opposite of what she'd been wearing. Heavy black boots, Doc Martens or an imitation, encased her feet. Tight black leggings with sinuous red stripes along the sides covered her lower half, and a long-sleeved black t-shirt covered the rest, with the words, "Come into my web, said the spider to the fly" in script letters above an anime spider.

She'd pulled her hair up into an off-center ponytail whose peak showed above her head, and her makeup was dramatic with red lips, sharp cheekbones, and black cat's eyes. As she walked toward the computer rig that dominated the space not taken up by the couch and the low table in front of it, Cait noticed Sabrina moved differently. She was more confident, more comfortable. The realization clicked with something the woman said during the team's night out, and Cait realized that the business version of Sabrina was also a costume. She was probably seeing the closest thing to the infomancer's true identity for the first time.

Sabrina crouched in front of a low cabinet, pulling it

open, and extracted a pair of headsets. She stood, closed its door, and handed the equipment over. "Advanced VR rigs. Wireless."

Cait accepted hers. "Nice couch. Nice room, in fact."

The other woman grinned. "Thanks. I have some special requirements. This atmosphere helps me work. Sometimes runs can be exhausting, so I need to sleep afterward, or I might not get home safely. Thus, the couch." Cait frowned, and Sabrina chuckled. "Don't worry. This shouldn't be that difficult, though."

As the infomancer sat and swiveled toward her computer, Aza said, *"I like her."*

Yeah. Me too. Garrett asked, "Anything on the ledger?"

Sabrina replied, "Still processing. My AIs are hammering on it, but it doubtless relies on either memory or a one-time pad, so the chances of brute force success are pretty small. Early results confirm that the last column is almost certainly money, and the first is a measure of intervals, likely days, from an arbitrary starting point. Given those, the middle is probably an ID code for people or businesses that he received money from or gave money to."

She pushed some buttons and the many displays in front of her lit up with a variety of information. A large curved one dominated the space immediately before her chair, with a vertical monitor on either side and two horizontal ones at the outermost points. "Of course, it could be he was a birdwatcher, the middle codes are bird genomes, and the last column is some sort of game money for a birdwatching competition." Her tone was somewhere between amusement and annoyance.

Cait replied, "But that's not likely."

The infomancer swiveled around and acknowledged, "Oh no, not at all. Just wanted to make clear that it could be anything at this point." She turned back to her computers, and her voice lost its playful edge.

"Okay, we know Meyer is problematic. We've got a warrant for his bank accounts, which you'd think would make life easy. Naturally, the bank is delaying handing over the data. That's the problem with in-house counsel. The company would be far more likely to roll over if they had to pay a lawyer's fee on an hourly basis."

Cait asked, "What does all that mean for us?"

She sensed Sabrina's grin. "That we do it the fun way. Here we go."

The image in her headset swirled and shifted as the infomancer did something with her technology, magic, or whatever. When it stabilized, Cait was in a bank vault filled with safe deposit boxes on three sides, some large, some small, all pristine. Each had a combination lock wheel on the front, along with holes for two keys. She asked, "Where are we?"

Sabrina replied, "Inside his bank's computer systems. Their infomancers' magic combines with mine to create a shared reality. They decided it would be a vault, and probably the choice to fill it with safe deposit boxes was theirs, too."

"So, what's your magic's part?"

"That the stuff contained in the boxes holding the data we want is gold coins rather than bills and papers."

Garrett asked, "How does that help?"

"Because I've got a friend who really likes money." Sabrina's avatar, which very much resembled her real-world looks, lifted a hand, and a figure popped into existence on top of it. It looked like the advertising icon for the *Monopoly* game, complete with a thick white mustache.

She said, "Go," and he floated through the air, examining each safe deposit box, moving methodically and rapidly through the room. When he finished, several of them were glowing. The infomancer muttered, "Oh, tricky."

Cait asked, "What?"

"The bank's infomancers did a good job hiding exactly where the data we seek is. Probably every safe deposit box in here is trapped or alarmed, except for the one we need. My bot was only able to narrow it down to these."

"Is that bad?"

Sabrina laughed. "It would be, except I'm better than them." She summoned another bot, this time a leprechaun, again inspired by Japanese animation.

Cait said, "Hey, watch the Irish jokes."

"It's not an Irish joke. He's my AI that's particularly attuned to gold. He takes longer to work than the other one, though, so I tend to use them as a pair." The leprechaun turned and bowed to Cait, winked, then flew through the air to examine each glowing box. When he finished, only a single box remained illuminated. Sabrina thanked him, and he vanished.

Garrett laughed. "I always think it's so weird when you do that."

The infomancer shrugged. "Someday the artificial intelligences might take over the world. I want to be on their good side when and if it happens." Her avatar stepped forward and lifted a hand, and the combination dial spun on its own. Two keys appeared and turned in the locks. She pulled out a bunch of gold and threw it into the air, where it vanished at the top of its arc.

Cait waited expectantly, and after what felt like it had been an hour but probably was only a couple minutes, asked, "So?"

Sabrina replied, "Nothing useful in there."

She sighed. "Damn. Guess the money's a dead end."

The other woman laughed, and in a passable Irish accent responded, "Ah, lass, we've only begun." Cait heard the *click* of a button, and the world in her VR helmet spun crazily.

CHAPTER EIGHTEEN

Sabrina drew a deep, centering breath as the whirl of transition ended. "You guys okay?"

From behind on her right, Garrett replied, "A little nauseated, thanks."

The new marshal, Cait, said, "Yeah. That was trippy."

Sabrina grinned. "No doubt. Welcome to Sabrina's joyride. Please keep your hands and feet in the car if you wish not to lose them."

The scenario surrounding them was her starting place on the magical dark web, a wide-open college campus courtyard filled with imaginary people playing Frisbee, sunbathing, and so forth. She'd never had that experience personally but had seen it in a movie once and thought it sounded fun. It helped her to get her mind where she wanted it to be.

She gestured at herself, and an approximation of Sherlock Holmes' overcoat and deerstalker cap appeared over her normal clothes. A dog materialized at her side, a bloodhound, and stared up at her. She nodded. "Yes, Spot. We're on the hunt."

She turned her hand, a gold coin appeared in it, and she flipped it in the air. It landed on the ground in front of the dog, and he sniffed it, making amusing grunts and snuffling noises as he thoroughly investigated it. He finally looked up at her and barked, and she vanished the coin. "Okay. Find it."

He raced forward, and she jogged beside him, his little legs keeping him at a pace she could easily match. In the real world, "Spot" was an artificial intelligence program she'd written specifically to track the movement of money. As they ran, the surrounding scenery changed.

Hard-edged seams transformed the surroundings as they proceeded through them, almost like rooms of different houses. From her construct, they moved into what she recognized as the English countryside north of London. Next was Tokyo, then Chicago, Rio, and Paris.

As they passed through more countries, she explained for the benefit of those behind her, "He's following an electronic money trail. The data we pulled gave him potential starting points, and somewhere along this path he's picked up the scent for real."

Finally, they burst out into a bright street with pedestrians walking on either side. Small cars whipped by as they barreled between their position and the beautiful Colonial building opposite. It had a pitched roof, multiple floors, and tall pillars supporting a separate cover that protected the stairs leading up to it.

Sabrina sighed. "We're in the Caymans. How original." Her avatar rolled its eyes. She knelt and patted the dog on the head. "Good boy, Spot." A dog biscuit appeared in her hand, and he ate it. She thanked him, and he vanished, along with her coat and hat. Rising, she gestured at the building ahead. "His money is in there. The bad news is a warrant won't work here. The worse news is that it's a real bank, not some rinky-dink operation, which means getting in and out without being noticed will be a challenge."

Cait asked, "Should we stop?"

Sabrina grinned. "Hell, no. I wanted to be sure you'd be appropriately impressed by my talents." She took her hands off the keyboard for a moment, cracked her knuckles, and rolled her neck.

She wasn't the kind of infomancer who could remain relaxed during a run, and she envied those people. For her, computer magic was exercise on the level of combat. It was also the best job she knew and one of the things she liked most. *So, you take the good with the bad. At least when I crash from exhaustion, I've earned the rest.*

She crossed the street carefully, moving into the alleyway between that building and the next. She noted the cameras above, charted their paths, and timed her move for when she'd be least likely to be noticed.

A gesture in the virtual world and a quick command in the real one summoned climbing spikes on her hands and feet. She scrambled up the wall, ascending between the columns of windows, quickly evading the view of the mounted cameras and reaching the roof.

Garrett said, "Damn, I love your style."

Sabrina replied, "You ain't seen nothing yet." He'd accompanied her on runs before, so she felt no need to impress him. The new marshal, though, didn't seem to have a lot of experience with infomancers. In Sabrina's mind, that meant she was *required* to show off, to represent the honor of all infomancer-kind. She stretched her hands up and meowed, and her clothes changed, becoming a replica of Catwoman's bodysuit, complete with pointed ears on the cowl. The outfit was part tool and part disguise, covering all of her, including her face.

Cait whispered, "Wicked."

She laughed. "Right?" The simulation's magic was strong, but as always, the scenario was a blend of her and them. She'd managed to insert a skylight into the setup. They'd trapped it. Fortunately, her costume carried a device to detect traps and a toolkit to deal with them once discovered. She disarmed the one on the skylight and used a suction cup and pointed claw to cut a hole in the glass large enough for her to fit through.

Sabrina attached a thin line to the skylight's metal structure, then swung inside, lowering herself carefully toward the bank building's lobby. She paused once her body was in, rotating slowly to identify all the cameras below, pointed at the floor. A pistol with a rectangular barrel was strapped to her left leg, and she drew it as quietly as possible to avoid detection by the audio sensors. She took careful aim and pulled the trigger, sending a small blob of putty across the room to stick onto the wall next to the camera.

The tiny electronic device inside put out a jamming signal, rendering the visual surveillance useless. She did the same with the other seven cameras that covered the space, then hit the button on the motor encased in her belt to resume her slow descent. Suspicion scratched at the corner of her mind, and she stopped before she reached the bottom, then tapped the side of her cowl to magnify her vision. The edge of the pressure plate that lay under her feet was barely there, imperceptible except to her many times increased visual detail. *Clever bastards. Double trapped the skylight.*

She started swinging gently, then hit the button to release the line when her arc was sufficient to carry her beyond the trap. She landed in a crouch with one hand on the floor, directly in the middle of a triangle of infrared beams. They littered the floor, but the eyepieces of her cowl showed her where they were. It was simply a matter of carefully stepping over, crawling under, or hurdling the barriers on the way to the large vault door in the rear.

In the real world, she wouldn't have been anywhere close to agile enough to pull it off. She probably could've done the swing and jump, but landing in a way that didn't send her falling into the beams was highly unlikely. Out there, she was somewhat gangly and possessed only average athletic ability, at best. In here, though, she was a veritable superhero.

Her therapist had suggested the appeal of being such a powerful virtual figure could be a detriment to her real life. Sabrina had only laughed and said, "I'm an infomancer. That *is* my real life. All of this is a waiting room." That statement had disquieted her therapist enough that she'd stopped going, turning to infomancer groups on the magical dark web for support instead and receiving it in abundance.

She jerked her attention back to the moment. "Okay. A couple more things, then we'll get serious." She took two small cylindrical objects about the size of her palm from a pouch on her belt and placed them on the floor. Pressing the buttons on their tops caused them to emit a field that would reflect sight and sound, prohibiting any noise or movement she made from being detected from the room she'd exited.

She held up both hands like she was pointing a rifle, and a heavy drill on a pair of wheeled tripods materialized. She rolled it forward to touch the vault and drilled into it.

Cait asked, "Isn't that cheating or something?"

Garrett replied, "I think it is. She does that kind of stuff all the time, though."

Sabrina said, "It's always possible to bend a simulation without breaking it since a combination of my magic and the enemy's creates it." *Who's hopefully not waiting for me in there.* The drill finished its work, and she swung the door open and entered. As soon as she was inside, the door slammed closed again with a loud *clank*, and two figures appeared in front of it. "Great, infomancers, not info-mancer. Awesome."

Her hands went back to her belt pouch. The left one came out with a pair of medium-sized silver metal orbs that filled her hand. She tossed them in the air, and they darted around the vault, collecting data. The other held a smoke bomb, and she threw it at her opponents' feet.

The vapor screen was specially designed for the virtual world and was essentially an attempt to hack the graphics capabilities of her foes' computers, which sometimes fell out of date even in the best infomancers' rigs. Staying abreast of the constant changes when you weren't willing to allow automatic updates, which no infomancer was, always proved a challenge for all but the most detail-oriented. *Or borderline obsessive-compulsive, like me.* Her hardware and software were pristine.

She dashed through the smoke toward the first enemy and leapt into the air, extended an arm, wrapped it around his throat, and slammed him to the floor as she landed. Her second opponent was already coming at her, denying her time to finish the first. She spun into a low leg sweep, which he jumped over.

He threw punches at her face, and she stumbled backward to avoid them. His avatar was using quick strikes reminiscent of karate moves. Her style was more similar to kung fu, and she blocked them with gentle movements that deflected them enough for her to remain unharmed.

On one of the blocks, she spun behind him and slammed an elbow into the back of his head, pitching him forward. The other had partially recovered from her earlier move and came at her. As he stepped into range, she lunged ahead and stabbed stiffened fingers into his throat. He coughed, choking, and she leapt at him for the second time, this time pistoning a sidekick into his face. His head slammed off the vault's metal side, and he hit the floor.

Sabrina spun and discovered the other one had pulled a pistol. A dart materialized in her palm, and she hurled it forward. It embedded itself perfectly in the barrel.

He stared at the weapon in astonishment, and she used the distraction to slide in, whip a crescent kick around to knock his arm out to the side, and stab her sudden claws, extended like Wolverine's, into his chest. He fell, still disbelieving. She looked down at him. "You're the one who decided to invoke something other than hands. Bad call."

She lifted her palm, and the orbs flew into it. To the man at her feet, she remarked, "This has been a White Hat test. Watch for the report." Then she disconnected and leaned back in her chair with a heavy sigh. "You guys can take your rigs off."

Cait asked, "White hat? What's that?"

Sabrina turned slowly in her chair and achieved verticality with a groan. "Infomancers group. Runs random security tests, then offers consulting services to vulnerable companies to help them improve their protection. I'll send the data in anonymously, minus a detail or two I can use if I want to break in again. Everybody wins, and we have deniability."

Garrett asked, "What did we find?"

Exhaustion swept over Sabrina, and she mumbled, "More coded information. It'll take a while to crack, but the bots are working on it." She waved. "Now get off my couch. I need a nap."

CHAPTER NINETEEN

The rest of the day was uneventful, and Cait managed an early evening nap beside Aza, her alarm set for an hour before midnight. When it rang, she dressed in dark exercise clothes, warned Aza to keep himself well hidden, and took him out for their nightly run.

Rather than the random path they'd taken before, Cait's route tonight had a specific purpose. One of Clement's informants, who he'd declined to identify, had shared the location of a bar where members of Rosetta's organization, the Roses, were known to hang out. She kept a measured pace, conserving her energy, her strengthened senses on the alert for trouble.

Aza swooped and soared above her, maintaining a steady flow of words in her head that frequently included *"Burn."* Rats, people, cars, and even a billboard that annoyed him all received dire threats from the dragon. She was careful not to let her amusement show. *He's a feisty one. The scary part is that he could light them on fire if he chose.*

After forty-five minutes, she reached her destination, a

block away from the club. She stopped running, leaned against a wall as she waited for her breathing to return to normal, and pulled the hood of her sweatshirt up, making sure it covered her hair. It only took a moment of focus to hear the conversations from the front of the building, where two large men in business suits managed a line of people waiting for their turn to enter.

Cait said quietly, "We're not going to get in the main door, that's for sure. I envisioned some kind of seedy bar, not a nightclub or whatever this is."

Aza, standing mostly invisibly beside her in the alley, replied in her head, *"We could burn our way in."*

She let out a soft snort. "Let's assume I always know burning will be your first choice, okay? Any other ideas?"

"Maybe we can go in the side door, like those guys."

Her eyes snapped up, peering into the alley across the street. It wasn't symmetrically opposite hers but offered an angle that allowed her to see people entering the building. A camera was mounted above the opening, covering the area. "No, still not sneaky enough."

Aza flapped his wings and launched into the air, his scales rippling to match the buildings as he rose, then shifting to dark so no one would see him against the night sky. After a few moments, he said, *"If you can get up to the roof over here, there's a path to the top of that building."*

She scowled. *If I can get to the roof. What's he think I am, a novice?* He gave her directions. She circled the building beside her and moved across the street with her back to the nightclub, headed in the opposite direction.

When she reached the appointed location, she used a force blast to send her up and landed cleanly on the roof.

All the structures in the area were three stories high, except for a few that only made it to two. The dragon led her on an indirect path that kept her on the taller buildings, most of the roofs close enough together that she could leap without magic.

Finally, they reached the top of the target building, coming at it from directly behind, where no obvious surveillance was in place other than a camera covering the street. She prowled the roof, walking over every part of it, pushing her enhanced senses to detect anything from below. In most of the area, the throb of loud music was the only thing she could get, but in one corner, she heard something different.

She laid flat on the pebbly roof and pressed her ear against its surface, ignoring the sticky sensation from the touch. Voices came from below, exclusively male, measured but annoyed. A man said, "The damned Dragons are encroaching on our territory in the south. We need to offer them an example of what happens when they cross the line."

Another voice asked, "How severe an example?"

The first chuckled. "We can stick to broken bones. Just a friendly caution, for now."

She whispered, "I wonder if that's Rosetta. Wish I had a bug."

Aza, who was looking at her from couple of feet away, replied, *"There are plenty around up here. Are you hungry? I could get you one."*

Cait stifled her laugh. "No, no. I don't need an actual bug. It's slang for a device I could put here to listen to them."

His head tipped in a nod. *"Oh. Well, since you don't have that, I could fly in through a window and burn them."*

She fought against the grin that kept trying to show itself. "No, I'm good."

"Really. I'm happy to."

"That's a little too bold a move right now."

A clear sigh came from her partner. *"But you'll let me know."*

She nodded, keeping her face frozen. "I will." The conversation from within the building continued, and she stood as one of the men inside indicated he was departing. "Let's try something. There's a guy who's leaving, and he's probably going to get in a car. I'm guessing he's important, so it will likely pull up in front of the club to pick him up. We'll stay up here until we see if that happens. If it does, you follow the man, and I'll do my best to follow you." She brushed off her clothes, then frowned. "No. Wait. I don't want you to wind up lost."

Aza, who had remained still during her movements, only his head moving to track her, replied, *"Impossible."*

She shook her head. "You don't know the city."

In a tone that sounded slightly exasperated, he insisted, *"We are connected. I can always find you."*

She blinked in surprise. "Let me try something." She opened all the senses she knew how to open, seeking some thread that bound them together, but failed to discover one. "Okay. Unfortunately, it doesn't seem to work the other way. So, we'll do it, and if I don't show up within a half-hour or so, you come back to me."

Aza nodded decisively. *"Good. One question. What's an hour?"*

Cait resisted the urge to rub her face with her hands. "If the sun comes up and I'm not with you, find me."

He gave her one of the grins she wasn't quite sure whether to identify as laughing with or laughing at. *"Perfect."*

The man came out and got into a car as she'd predicted, and Aza flew after it. Cait pushed magic into her muscles to increase her speed and jumping ability, then leapt from one rooftop to the next. She couldn't see the vehicle but kept an eye on the dragon, who had wisely left part of his upper scales uncamouflaged so she could see them.

She would've never been able to keep up if they hadn't been in the city, but the car ran into a lot of red lights along the way, allowing her to make up ground at each pause. Finally, Aza hovered rather than continuing forward. When she reached him, he said, *"They are inside that building."*

She peered over the edge of the roof and saw a large warehouse. A dilapidated sign along the side said Casale Cheese Company. "Okay, come on down." A moment later, he landed beside her. "So, he went in there?"

"Yes. With whoever else was in the car. The whole car did."

"Makes sense. Safer that way and that place is huge." Her experienced eye reviewed the building's security and noted it had far more cameras than it should.

"No chance of breaking in there without better equipment and planning. Still, we've learned something important tonight. We have two places where we know we can find the Roses. Maybe next time, we'll be able to follow someone from here and get another."

Aza locked eyes with her and shook his head. *"Boring*

plan. I have a better one. Break in. Flames for anyone who fights us. Demand answers from the rest."

This time she couldn't contain her laugh and smiled down at him. "You're kind of aggro, bud."

He grinned. *"Of course. I'm a dragon."*

CHAPTER TWENTY

Wednesday and Thursday passed without any new information. Cait spent her days doing typical marshal stuff. She investigated Judge Meyer's killing, got acquainted with prisoner transport procedures, which were pretty much the same as those in Columbus, and continued to acquaint herself with the faces of fugitives suspected to be in the region.

Clement took her out once to show her some of the back streets, and she did the rounds of police stations with Bradley, meeting some more of his most trusted acquaintances. Friday finally arrived, and the opportunity to meet with Leonard Rosetta, the purported leader of the Roses criminal organization.

She dressed in her best business wear, another dark suit, but with a masculine button-down shirt underneath. It was purple, her only touch of style. Aza shrank to the appropriate size, leapt from the bed to her shoulder, then climbed under her hair, nuzzling and tickling the back of her neck until she laughed. Then he coiled around and transformed into the necklace, blinking gemstone eyes once before becoming inert. She remarked, "It is so weird watching you do that."

His voice held amusement. *"Good."*

She met Bradley in front of one of the larger structures in Boston, a skyscraper whose exterior was all glass, reflecting the sky and the other buildings around. The only obvious security personnel in the lobby were a couple of blue-uniformed guards with pistols on one hip and Tasers on the other. Cameras looked down from several angles, and she imagined in a place that held the kind of monied businesses this one did, a more heavily armed response team was also present somewhere in the facility. *Not likely they'd rely on public resources for their clients' sense of well-being.*

They checked in at the large semicircular reception desk and received visitors' tags with the instruction to tap them on the reader in the elevator, which would take them where they needed to go. They did so and rode it up to the seventy-first floor, about three-quarters of the way to the top, she guessed. The doors opened onto an elevator lobby, and glass doors ahead declared that they'd reached the law offices of Sherman, Glass, and Burke. She said, "Wow. I guess they have the whole floor?"

Garrett replied, "Unless there's a separate set of elevators that serves another part of the floor, yeah, I'm guessing so."

"Impressive."

"Would you have expected less, given who we're meeting?"

She held her visitor tag up to a sensor beside the door,

and it unlocked. She pulled it open and gestured for her partner to go in first. "I guess not."

A receptionist stood at the front desk inside, his suit likely as expensive as anything she owned, from the look of it. He said, "Ms. Chandler will be with you in a moment." He didn't offer refreshments, or the opportunity to sit, which she took to mean they weren't necessarily welcome guests. *No matter where you are, some things never change.*

A woman in an even more expensive-looking suit came down a hallway and extended her hand to each of them, introducing herself as the person the receptionist told them to expect. She offered a plastic smile. "Please follow me."

She led them to a small room, about the size of a large walk-in closet, with a half-dozen tall wooden lockers in elegant mahogany with gold appointments. Each had a key in its lock, attached by a chain to a metal rectangle with a number engraved on it. The lawyer instructed, "You will need to remove all your jewelry and weapons except your service revolver. Also, your footwear."

Cait turned to regard her. "Seriously?"

The woman offered a thin smile, and Cait sensed that she was enjoying herself. "If you wish to meet with Mr. Rosetta, yes."

"Why?"

The woman's nostrils flared as she expelled a breath, signaling mild annoyance. "You are both carrying pistols. Be grateful we're not asking you to go against that regulation. As for the rest, you, Marshal Bradley, have an edged weapon of some sort in your shoe and a switchblade in your pocket. Very naughty, by the way. I believe those are illegal in the state."

The woman returned her attention to Cait. "Your bracelet and necklace read as potentially magical. Your earrings probably aren't, but we won't take the risk of being wrong about that." Her thin smile reappeared. "We do have slippers for you in the lockers. One-size-fits-all."

Cait scowled and exchanged glances with Garrett. She shrugged and shook her head but complied. As she removed Aza from around her neck and set the necklace into the locker next to her bracelet, he offered, *"This can't hold me if I want to get out. If you need me, scream."*

She gave a slight nod and closed the door after retrieving the surprisingly comfortable slippers. They followed the lawyer into a spacious office with couches and a low table at one end and a large desk at the other, empty except for a legal pad and a computer keyboard. The man sitting in the chair behind it was slim and dressed in a light-colored suit with a white button-up shirt open at the throat. His expertly styled hair was black salted with gray. His mustache matched, perfectly sculpted, not reaching his lip, clean lines all around.

He rose and nodded at Garret as they reached the opposite side of the desk. "You, I know of Marshal Bradley." He turned a smile on her. "But you," he extended his hand, gently grabbed hers, and lifted it to his lips, "I do not. I'm confident that if I'd seen you before, I'd remember." His words were courtly, even flirty.

She replied, "Deputy US Marshal Cait Keane. My pleasure, Mr. Rosetta."

"Definitely mutual, then." He gestured. "Sit, please, let's

talk." As he lowered himself into his chair, a man in a suit delivered a silver tray with bottles of sparkling water to the desk. Rosetta took one, screwed off the cap, and sipped it, tipping the bottle toward them to suggest they should do the same.

He said, "Before you ask, I didn't give the order for Judge Meyer's death. Not that I didn't have a reason. He was a right bastard that never had an impartial day on the bench, at least not in this city. But the word didn't come from me."

Garrett suggested, "One of your underlings, then."

Rosetta waved as though to banish the thought. "If so, they're freelancing. If you discover that's the case, whisper the name to me, and it won't be a problem any longer."

Cait frowned. "Are you asking us to join in a considered criminal conspiracy?"

The man across the desk burst into laughter. "No, no. I'm asking you to warn me if you find that someone in my organization is acting unprofessionally and should be fired."

She repeated dryly, "Fired."

He nodded. "I won't have untrustworthy people in my employ, Ms. Keane. Or is it Mrs.?"

She squashed a grin. Despite the fact that he was likely a very bad man, he was still charming in a way that reminded her of her father. "Marshal will do."

Rosetta gave a minimal shudder but smiled. "So reserved, so cold."

Bradley asked, "If not you," he paused as the man on the opposite side of the desk gestured. "I mean, if not one of your people freelancing, who do you think it might have been?"

"My first line of investigation were I you, would be the Dragons. They're the ones who turn to violence at the drop of a hat." He chuckled darkly. "Or the snap of a fortune cookie, if you prefer."

The casual racism caused her word to come out more harshly than she would've liked. "*Really*?"

His eyes showed that he recognized his provocation had struck its target. "Certainly. Check with local authorities. They'll back me up on that."

Garrett asked, "Which ones are on your payroll?"

Rosetta laughed, reclining in his chair and pointing at the other marshal. "Good one, Bradley. All of them, of course. Doughnuts and coffee every morning. Being a good citizen has its rewards."

The lawyer intervened, stepping forward, perhaps at some nonverbal cue from Rosetta. "This interview is at an end, Marshals. If you require anything else from my client, send your request through me."

They rose, and Cait smiled at Rosetta. "Until we meet again, Mr. Rosetta."

He stood, snagged her hand, and kissed it. "I hope it's soon, Deputy US Marshal Cait Keane." Then he turned and nodded at her partner. "Mr. Bradley."

Garrett replied, "Mr. Rosetta."

They retrieved their gear in silence and made it out to the elevator lobby. As they stepped into the lift, Garrett said, "Let me guess. You're never going to wash that hand again. Do you need me to catch you? Are you about to swoon?"

She laughed and finished putting in her second earring. "Bite me, Garrett."

He grinned. "I'm a married man, Keane. Keep it in your pants."

She snorted, shook her head, but didn't give him the satisfaction of a reply. In her mind, Aza said, *"He's funny. I like him."*

She watched the floor numbers count down in silence. *I think Leonard Rosetta is going to turn out to be big trouble.*

CHAPTER TWENTY-ONE

Late that night, after a nap, Cait grabbed her bag and opened a portal to her other home. She stepped through with Aza at her side, switching from night to day in only a single stride. She banished the portal behind her and waited, one hand on the dragon's shoulder where he sat beside her. He was about the size of a German Shepherd, which was about what he'd been for most of their nighttime runs. Three witches emerged from the house all at once. Her mother held a wand in her hand, Brianna carried a shillelagh, and Aisling gripped a wooden sword, her practice weapon. Cait raised a palm. "It's all good. You can relax."

Brianna said, "We sensed something weird."

Aisling added, "It was clearly you because it couldn't have been that *gorgeous* creature beside you."

Aza laughed in her mind. "Everyone, this is Aza. Aza, this is my mother, Moira, my sister, Brianna, and my other sister, Aisling."

Her family members came in one by one, patting the

dragon and allowing him to sniff them, treating him like an animal they were meeting for the first time. He made amusing comments in her mind while they did so, but clearly enjoyed the attention. Moira said, "Well, two more for breakfast, then. What does your friend eat?"

She laughed. "Meat or fish, well cooked."

Aza said, *"I can help with the last part."*

She sighed. "He's offering to help cook the food. I'd be careful though. His idea of cooking seems to be more super-well-done than medium if you catch my drift."

Aisling frowned. "I didn't hear him say anything."

In her mind, Aza said, *"She's the smart one, I guess?"*

She smacked him gently. "We're all smart." She looked back at her family. "He talks telepathically to me. No, before you ask, I can't do the same to him. Also, before you ask, I don't know if he can do it with anyone else. If he does, be sure to tell me. And my apologies in advance."

Aza commented, *"Ha. You're funny."*

They went inside and shared a satisfying breakfast of oatmeal and the trimmings, plus some leftover smoked fish for the dragon, which he ate greedily. Afterward, they headed out to the backyard to chat and relax. After a while, Brianna asked, "How good is he in a fight?"

The dragon replied instantly, *"Excellent."*

Cait laughed. "His opinion is that he's quite good. We haven't yet fought together or against each other." She was reluctant to speak of the trial she'd undergone to find him, and her family must have sensed it since they didn't ask.

Instead, Aisling said, "I'll get my other sword. Let's find out for ourselves."

As she rushed inside, accompanied by their mother,

Cait explained to Aza, "We spend a lot of time sparring, practice fighting."

He lowered his head in a nod. *"My family and I do the same."*

"Do you think you can join in without causing us damage?"

"Of course. I'm quite skilled. I'll keep my claws in."

"And no fire."

The dragon heaved a heavy sigh. *"Fine."* He smiled as he said it.

A couple of minutes later, she and her sisters were in a circle around Aza, her mother watching from near the house. Cait and Brianna held their practice shillelaghs, and Aisling gripped a sword in each hand. Cait observed, "It seems impractical, cutting yourself off from being able to cast like that with both hands full."

Her sister shrugged. "It's only training. I like the way it feels. Plus, most of the techniques you practice with two, you can use with one."

"What does Delsanra say about that?"

She scowled and imitated their teacher. "That practice is life." Her voice returned to normal. "Apparently, I shouldn't be enjoying it."

Brianna burst into laughter. "Well, that certainly sounds like him."

Cait grinned. "Ready, Aza?"

In response, the dragon lunged at her. She snapped her weapon across in a light blow to intercept him, and he stopped suddenly and rolled quickly to one side, coming up to his feet across from Aisling. He whipped his tail around, forcing Brianna to block before he knocked her legs out from underneath her.

He snapped at Cait's youngest sister, who interposed a sword to prevent his teeth from reaching her. Then the melee was on in earnest. Each of them attacked whenever an opening presented itself. The dragon understood the purpose of the practice because she was sure he was deliberately giving them opportunities to strike. Their blows landed lightly when they made it through his defenses, and when he connected with a swat to her side, it barely knocked Cait off-balance.

Things shifted when he took to the air, swooping down in telegraphed attacks that still turned out to be hard to counter. He puffed vapor from his nostrils on one such attack, and murmured in her mind, *"You're on fire."* He performed the same against each of her sisters, saying, *"And so is she. Her, too."*

They continued until their muscles grew tired, then lay on the grass in the sun, resting and talking. Aza was stretched out on his back, all four paws in the air, lying with his head on her legs. Her sisters caught her up on the coven's news from the last week, which included the discussions and politicking her mother had predicted around the question of new leadership. Once they'd adequately rested, they surveyed the garden together, concluding that it was coming along nicely.

The morning slipped by in a haze of pleasant enjoyment until their mother called them in for lunch. The family threw questions at Aza while they ate, requiring her to translate his answers between hasty bites of food. They discovered that he didn't have much information to share, except that he was part of a group of dragons of many ages and sizes and that he was the youngest when he left.

Cait said, "He was bigger than a horse when I met him." She spread her arms wide to illustrate the point.

Aisling asked Aza, "Can all dragons shift size?"

He shook his head slowly and answered in Cait's mind, *"I'm not sure. I only know that I can do it. It doesn't seem special to me."*

It took Cait a couple of minutes to realize that one of the smaller stones in her bracelet had started to heat up, the growing pain finally catching her attention. She threw her napkin on the table with a sigh. "Sashura calls. I'll see you all later. Aza, you might as well come with me, but keep an eye on how to get back here in case she doesn't want you to stay."

They left by the front door, and Cait led the dragon into the wooded area that broke the oval of houses. He asked, *"Who is Sashura, and why does she get to decide whether I stay or not? Seems like she needs a lesson. With fire."*

Cait laughed. "Fire is not the answer to every question."

"It can be."

She shook her head and reached down to run her palm along his back. "I guess I can't argue with that. But please, no burning my teacher, at least not until after I've properly introduced you."

CHAPTER TWENTY-TWO

They reached the clearing where her teacher waited for her after a short walk. The space wouldn't have held more than maybe twenty people comfortably, and small, new trees broke through the ground in several places. The center of the expanse was a large stone disc with concentric metal circles running at intervals inside it. It was a place for training in magic, and the wards provided protection when working with dangerous spells.

Cait approached her teacher. The woman was willowy and didn't match her years, with fair skin and dark hair showing no age signs. Her face was wide and honest, but her eyes were the most notable feature. They were sharp, incisive, and unyielding, a brilliant blue. Cait gestured at her companion. "This is Azasainia, Aza for short."

Sashura gave the dragon a slight bow. "It is my pleasure to meet you, Aza."

Cait replied, "And his, to meet you."

Her teacher's eyes returned to her. "He speaks to you telepathically?" She nodded. "Interesting."

"Is it possible to teach me telepathy, so I can do the same back to him?"

Sashura gestured with the thin wand she held in her right hand, then stared at them for several seconds. "Perhaps, when the connection between you deepens. Your auras are still too dissimilar for such magic."

Shoving away her disappointment, Cait replied, "What shall I learn today, *meantóir?*" It was the way their sessions always started.

The other woman tapped her wand into the open palm of her empty hand, considering them. "That the spirits have called you is concerning. That they have seen fit to provide you with a partner, even more so."

Cait replied, "The fox, my guide, said danger was coming. For me, or the coven, or both. It was a little unclear."

Sashura nodded. "I cannot see what lies ahead. Sadly, that magic has long been lost to us." Her teacher was descended from the most powerful witches of the coven, stretching back for generations. Once identified, those women were duty-bound to find equally gifted partners to ensure the magic flowed as strong or stronger to their children. "It seems likely that you will need protection beyond what your magic currently provides. So, today, you shall learn a fused shield."

Cait frowned, never having heard of such a thing. "As you wish, teacher." Sashura gestured, and Cait moved into the circle. Aza wisely stayed off the stone. A tingle in her back signaled that her teacher had called up the outermost ward.

Without warning, the other woman threw a fireball at

Cait. She summoned a shield of ice, meeting the attack halfway between them, and the elements canceled each other out in a flash of steam. Her teacher conjured ice next, and she countered with fire. Lightning met force, then force met force.

Sashura frowned at her. "I can sense your instinctive response to each attack is force magic. It is to your credit that you overcame it on the first two attacks. But this predictability is not wise."

"It works best against bullets."

Her teacher's lips twisted in a slight scowl. "Nonetheless, you must resist developing a default choice and make the optimal decision for the moment. You will doubtless face things more dangerous than bullets."

Well, isn't that a lovely thought? Cait nodded. "Yes, teacher."

Sashura said, "Close your eyes and focus your will. I want you to create a force bubble around you." She complied, and the other woman instructed, "Now, a lightning shield outside it."

It required her to split off a portion of her mind to maintain the first barrier while the rest focused on summoning the next. Casting two spells at once was something she often did, and she accomplished the task easily.

"Now, merge them."

She frowned. "Like, half-and-half?"

Sashura shook her head. "No. All and all. A single barrier of magic, but made of force and lightning, intertwined so closely that they are essentially one."

Cait tried but was unable to produce the requested magic. Her teacher clucked her tongue. "This is what comes of your dependence upon force. Take my words to heart, Caitriona."

Sashura stepped forward and laid a gentle hand on her cheek. She felt pressure in her mind, guiding her along the path to accomplish the magic the other woman demanded. That magical mental ability resulted from decades of working together and still could not outright teach her new things. It could only assist her in finding her way.

After several minutes of internal effort that felt like running in an all-out sprint, she accomplished it. She opened her eyes to see the slight glimmer of the force magic and the overlapping sparkle of electricity. Sashura remarked, "Good. Very good. You've reached the first stage. Now, without losing what you've created, add ice."

Although logic would suggest she should be able to do so more quickly, now that she'd achieved it once, it took her twice as long to add the third element to her protective barrier. When she finished, she let the magic fall, unable to maintain the trio of spells any longer, much less work to add whatever other features Sashura might demand. "That was exhausting. I feel like I'm empty of every kind of energy."

"Understandable. You may sit."

She did, dropping into a crossed-legged posture. Aza came up behind her, leaning his body against hers, and she realized her teacher must have dispelled the ward.

Sashura had adopted a mirrored position across from her. "You will need to begin actively developing your *draíocht* pool to its full capacity."

Cait frowned. The other woman had never mentioned

that her reservoir of magic was lacking before. "It's not already?"

Her teacher offered a small headshake. "No. You have great potential and can reach lofty heights if you do the work to reach it."

Cait scowled. "Don't say it."

Sashura smiled. "You don't practice enough, Caitriona."

She sighed, closed her eyes, and tilted her face toward the sun. "I asked you not to say that."

Aza offered, *"I could burn her."*

She bumped him with her shoulder but said to her teacher, "I'm not sure I can maintain this kind of shield and also attack."

Sashura replied, "You shall need to develop that skill. It will come with practice. You have my word. You'll also require a second wand."

Cait opened her eyes and stared across at the other woman. "What? That's a thing?"

"Yes."

"Okay. Cool, then. Will do." Inwardly, she thought, *Why the hell am I only hearing about this now? More magic and a second wand could have been useful, I don't know, always.*

Her teacher said, "Tomorrow, you may choose what you wish to learn, and I will teach it."

Cait sighed. "I'm sorry. I won't be here tomorrow. This is a quick trip, and unfortunately, I have other obligations to meet."

Sashura inclined her head, and Cait imagined the unspoken words, "You don't practice enough, Caitriona." But her teacher only said, "Next time, then."

The exertions required her to take a nap, and, of course, Aza was more than willing to sleep. Again, despite his ability to shift to any size, he seemed to prefer being big enough to make it difficult for both of them to fit in the bed. She shoved him, he pushed her, and finally, they fell asleep. They slept through dinner and only rose when Brianna woke them with barely sufficient time remaining to get ready for the meeting.

She dressed in the same outfit as the prior week, and Aza transformed into the necklace to avoid becoming a distraction. She patted his metallic-looking neck and felt scales. "We'll get you a proper introduction next time, my friend."

He replied sleepily, *"Okay. I already know all the important people."* Loyalty radiated from him as it had since the moment he'd laid in her arms and whispered, "Mine." She wasn't sure she'd ever had another person who had been so devoted to her, and it was equal parts heartwarming and fear-inducing. *That's a lot to live up to.*

The circle's dynamics had changed by the time they were all arranged. Instead of being opposite Sinead and her daughters, Cait's mother, sisters, and Cait were across from another family, a mother and two daughters.

Sinead stepped forward and led them through the lighting ceremony her mother had performed at the last gathering. When it was complete, the soon to be replaced leader said, "I have been reliably informed that the coven's members have asked two families to consider becoming our leaders." She gestured at the others, named them, then did the same for Cait's family. "Would either of you wish to withdraw your acceptance of this great honor?"

The matriarch of the other family was quick to snap, "We do not."

Cait's mother calmly replied, "Nor do we."

Sinead smiled as if that was the answer she'd expected. "All of you have had time to discuss the important issues before us this week. The moment is at hand for us to come to a decision." She waved her wand and sketched symbols in the air, whispering an invocation. Above their heads, one directly over each family, a pair of spheres materialized, glowing gently. Sinead said, "Now, sisters, declare your choice."

Like the other coven members, Cait extended her power into the surrounding forest. She found what she was looking for and urged it to come to her bidding. The firefly was happy to comply and flew out into the clearing. Cait's focus was on her representative, but she saw the same thing happening all around, the twinkling insects flowing forward at the request of the coven. Only the witches were allowed to vote. Partners and guests had no permission to join in the decision.

The fireflies coalesced into the spheres, darting around inside, blinking in irregular patterns, and seemingly playing together. As more of the insects gathered, the orbs grew brighter. By the time the last insect had found its place, the one over Cait's family's head was notably more brilliant than the Mohans'. Sinead said, "Our decision is made. Moira Keane and her daughters will lead the coven." She clapped, and the spheres exploded into fireworks. The fireflies flew, played, and danced as they left the clearing.

Cait followed her mother as she walked over to Lyla Mohan. Moira said, "Thank you for your willingness to lead. I hope you will support us, as we would have you."

The woman spoke sharply. "Of course." Then she and her daughters turned and stalked away. Moira turned to face Cait and her sisters. "Well. I'm going to go out on a limb and say we can't depend on them."

Brianna laughed. "You think?"

Aza muttered, *"I could burn them for you."*

Cait echoed the offer, and Moira chuckled. "Not yet, my newest child, and hopefully not ever. But it's good to know that if things turn dark, you are there for my daughter and the rest of us."

Once again, Cait executed a quick clothing change, then led Aza downstairs for goodbyes. Her family made a big deal of hugging him and wishing him well, and he ate up every moment of it. When they finished, she announced, "He said he loves you too, but you're all insane." Brianna hit her, and she admitted having made the second part up. Then it was her turn for hugs.

As she closed the door behind them, he said, *"I like it here."*

"Me too. I bet you're going to love meeting Patrick." She headed toward the path that would take them up the mountain, so she could rest and refresh before the challenges the next day would bring. *I'll need all the rest I can get before SOG training tomorrow.*

CHAPTER TWENTY-THREE

Cait's membership in the US Marshals' Special Operations Group had been one of the parts of her job she'd most enjoyed since becoming part of the service several years before. The training and qualifying had been brutal, but she'd conquered it and earned a place in the elite tactical unit. At first, she'd only worked with the regional response team. Later, after distinguishing herself there, she'd become fully part of the national team. They'd added a second unit and a third, assigning each a geographic area to cover.

Hers was still the original, based out of the Marshals' Service Tactical Operations Center at Camp Beauregard in Louisiana. The camp was a sprawling Army base, with areas devoted to the Marshals, the National Guard, and other special units. Her team occupied a single ops building, and she'd arranged to have a closet kept empty and locked, only able to be opened from the inside. She portaled to that location, ensuring a safe and subtle arrival, then paused before opening the door. "Okay, Aza, time to do your jewelry impression."

"Are you sure? I'd make a great teammate."

She laughed. "You're already a great teammate, but one I want to keep as my secret weapon."

The dragon gave a small snort and jumped, shrinking to the size of a squirrel before landing on her arm. He crawled up it, his claws digging into her skin, reducing himself to the stature of a chipmunk by the time he reached her spine. Then he flowed and changed into the necklace.

Over time, she'd realized that he didn't change in substance. He was still a living and very slowly breathing dragon around her neck. He simply used his camouflage to appear as jewelry. *Yeah, simple, right.* She wondered momentarily if thermal imaging would detect him, then figured his magic probably addressed that issue. She hoisted her duffel bag over her shoulder and exited the room.

The building was military standard, with linoleum floors and bright fluorescent lights along aesthetically displeasing but functional hallways. She followed one to the locker rooms, checking her watch. Fifteen minutes remained before she had to be in a specific place.

The members of her team who were residents on the base would get dressed in their barracks or quarters. Most of them would've come the night before to share some social time. She'd have to buy a round of drinks after the day's session to make up for her absence.

Her lack of availability kept her slightly apart from the

others. She worked hard to negate any disconnect by reaching out to each of them every couple of days by text or email, ensuring they were part of one another's lives even when they weren't together.

She spun the combination and opened the locker door. She threw her civilian clothes into the duffel and shoved it into the top part of the locker, ramming it until it fit. Three uniforms hung inside, forest camo, desert camo, and night black.

She withdrew the first and donned it quickly, grabbed boots from the locker's bottom and secured them after tucking her pant legs inside against whatever muck they'd wind up walking through. She snagged the matching helmet, the customized goggles sized specifically for her head and face, her bulletproof vest, and the thin cover that would make the body armor match the rest of the outfit.

Cait arrived in the briefing room two minutes before the start, closer than she preferred to cut it. It still gave her time to pull a cup of coffee from a carafe in the corner and throw her gear on a seat at the edge of the second row. As the others funneled in, she exchanged fist bumps and hugs, depending on her connection to them.

Last to arrive was Commander Elliott Black, tall and imposing with a high and tight military hairstyle. His age could have been anything from twenty-five to forty, based on his looks. He went straight for the podium and called, "All right, settle down, people. We have work to do today." Since only six individuals were in the room, the other half of their full team must be out on separate training. Every third or fourth session was like that.

The team's operation and intel specialist, Tori Lawson, replied, "When don't we, boss?"

He smiled thinly. "True. But you're going to like today's gig."

From the back of the room, where she stood next to medical expert Kingston Foster, Julie Schor called, "Well, don't keep us in suspenders, boss." The stupid joke got more groans than laughs, and Elliot shook his head.

"If you weren't such a good engineer, Schor, I'd put you right out of the unit for your insubordination." She returned a saucy smile, and he laughed. Their high-functioning team could insult and threaten each other with impunity when not on a mission, and no one took offense as long as it didn't get *too* insubordinate.

For Cait, who was still feeling her way into the connections and relationships in her new office, it was like having a second family. It energized her, and she was sure the exercise to come would do the same.

Elliot said, "Today we're going to give a National Guard unit a little surprise." A couple of people clapped, and he continued, "Their commander reached out. He thought we might be able to provide them with a more realistic understanding of the need for perimeter defense."

His smile had a predatory edge. "They're in the forest and won't be expecting our visit. It should be a cakewalk, assuming you grunts don't screw it up."

More laughter. Angel Morello, the team's expert on seemingly every weapon in existence, called, "We using the good stuff?"

Elliot shook his head. "Paintball gear. Watch your shots because they might not all be goggled."

Angel scowled and crossed his arms. The muscles in them bulged beneath his brown skin. He was the one they expected would be the last one standing in any pitched battle. "We need some of that cool electronic training gear. Like laser tag, only better."

Cait called, "You need a lot of things, Angel. A brain, first and foremost."

He grinned and retorted, "Sure, Sabrina." Alone among her colleagues, Angel felt comfortable making jokes about her magical nature and usually picked a fictional witch at random as her moniker for the day. He'd confused the rest of the team once by calling her Morgaine, demonstrating that he had a much wider intellectual scope, at least in literature, than they'd given him credit for. She'd recognized the reference, of course.

Elliot ordered, "Pair up for gear check." They pulled on their full uniforms, strapping on vests and drawing paintball guns from the crate wheeled into the room by a staff member during the briefing. Each had at least a rifle and pistol. Julie, the team's engineer and communication expert, had additional packs holding heaven only knew what.

They gathered outside the building when they were ready to go, and Elliot nodded in satisfaction. "Okay, people. We are on mission as of now. Form up, and let's get to the trees."

They ran two abreast, with Elliot moving up and down the line as they jogged the mile to the part of the base where the forest encroached. It was a large, wooded area with acres and acres of undeveloped land that provided the units with ample space to train. Cait spent one week of her vacation each year with the team, working in other environments, a grueling experience that reminded them all of their initial training. She loved it.

Aza said in her mind, *"It would be faster to portal."*

She couldn't argue. The inclusion of magicals in the SOG was still a work in progress. While her superiors were willing to take advantage of the opportunities she could provide in moments of crisis, training was always magic-free, or at least mostly so. In any case, it would never be used for something as pedestrian as physical comfort. That word didn't appear in the dictionaries of the SOG teams.

When they reached the forest's edge, Elliot, call sign Knight, split them into pairs. As usual, she teamed with Angel, whose call sign, appropriately, was Devil. They were assigned point, and she whispered the spell to activate her enhanced senses.

She wished it was magic she could bestow on another, but to be honest, Angel's raw skill closed most of that gap. They raised fists simultaneously at a sound from ahead where there shouldn't be one. The other two teams, behind to the right and left, shifted into cover. He murmured, "Going up?"

She nodded. He pulled a thin cable from his equipment belt, attached a carabiner to the end, then threw it up and over the nearest branch. He lowered the line. She secured it to her belt and moved to the tree. With his assistance and her strong climbing ability, she scaled it with ease.

Aza replied, *"You could fly."*

She whispered, "Have to learn to do things without magic, too, my friend."

"I don't."

She chuckled. *Guess not, since it's your nature.* "Well, I do." She pressed the button to switch her goggles to thermal imaging and saw bodies a short distance ahead, their temperatures different enough from their surroundings that the gear could pick them out from her high angle viewpoint.

She tapped a command on the comm device strapped to her arm to send that image to her team. In her earpiece, Elliot whispered, "Oh, an ambush with people they're not supposed to have. Someone's looking to have some fun with us. Well, let's oblige them."

She slid down the line, and Angel stowed his cable. They advanced into position, waiting while the others did the same. The National Guard sentries had deployed in pairs, but they'd been co-located rather than positioned apart to support one another. It would be easier to take both out simultaneously without revealing themselves. Unlike the guardsmen's weapons, her team's rifles had suppressors like the ones they took into the field often did.

Elliot gave the command. With soft noises of expelled air, each National Guard sentry received three orbs of paint between chest and legs since they were shooting lower than normal as instructed. The victims set their weapons down quietly, per the rules of training engagements, lowered themselves to sitting positions, and removed their radios.

Cait and her team advanced, scanning with thermal vision and her enhanced senses, sure that another line of sentries awaited them. Julie, call sign Crystal, hissed, "Freeze. Tripwire."

Their leader said, "They've gone all-out. It won't be long until our 'kills' miss a comm check. Keep your eyes out for traps, but get moving double time. No stopping until we win, or we're dead."

CHAPTER TWENTY-FOUR

They discovered more tripwires as they moved through the forest and eventually found and removed the next layer of the ambush team. As they neared the clearing their intel said the National Guard unit occupied, they noted the presence of a cluster of sentries to the north and south of the cleared area. The guardsmen were holding defensive positions, probably in hastily dug trenches. Julie grinned. "I've got something for that. Devil, you take the ones on the far side."

Angel replied, "On it," and accepted a bag from her. The rest of them crouched, took swigs from their canteens, and made sure their rifles were fully loaded. With a pair of loud *pops,* grenades went off, covering the defensive emplacements in color.

Two more sounded immediately afterward, and Julie remarked, "Outstanding. Fortunately, they were wearing goggles, so we could use indiscriminate methods."

Kingston Foster, call sign Royal, chuckled. "Indiscriminate indeed." Even though he was the team's medic and wore a custom backpack and several pouches, he also carried a rifle and was a fully combat-ready team member. *Who appreciates grenades.*

Elliott ordered, "Before we go out into the open, look for snipers."

Angel replied, "Do sniper paintball weapons exist?"

Their leader, off to her right, shrugged. "Lots of surprises already today. Could be more."

There was a surprise, but not a sniper. Their radios crackled, and someone said, "We're in the cabin. We've got a hostage."

Elliott snapped, "Switch to Channel B." Cait pressed the appropriate button on the comm armband. He continued, "Channel A will be me talking to the enemy. You can listen, but no transmission. We have to assume they're covering the logical lines of approach, probably with guns in the windows. Spirit, time to use your mojo."

Cait replied, "If there's a magical in there, they might be able to detect a veil or any other illusion I use to get close, which would give up the game."

Elliott paused for a second, then responded, "Everyone except Devil and Spirit with me. We'll move around to the left and try to keep their attention on us. You two sneak to the other side and see what you can make work. Clearly, we won't be able to negotiate them out in this training scenario. So, when you're ready for action, let me know."

Cait said, "Devil, let's meet halfway." He clicked in affirmation, and she moved toward him, staying in the trees. When they met, she activated the magnification in her goggles, staring at the back of the cabin. It had one window up high, and another symmetrically placed on the first level. "That matches what we saw on the side as we came in."

He replied, "And what I saw on the far side. So, identical, maybe with extra windows in the front."

"Second floor seems dicey."

"Concur."

Cait frowned, considering her options. "Got anything useful on you?"

Angel grinned. "Smoke grenade."

"Didn't know that was part of today's loadout."

"Some things you've just gotta have, no matter what."

Aza observed, *"Smoke is good. Fire is better. We could give them a* real *surprise."*

She tried not to let her laugh escape. "Best plan I've got is Knight distracts from the front. We use the grenade as a distraction to the side and rush the back."

He nodded. "Works for me. I shoot, you magic?"

"Seems like the only viable option."

Angel checked his rifle, tested to ensure that his pistol was ready to be drawn, then said, "Good to go."

Cait summoned her focus and whispered the words to craft an illusion around them, one that she would have to concentrate to maintain since they would be moving, requiring constant shifting in what it showed.

Fortunately, she'd had years and years of illusion practice with her sisters, playing the magical version of hide-and-seek that was far more difficult than the non-magical one. She said, "Knight, start your distraction," tapped her partner's arm, and advanced. As they passed the halfway point, he threw the grenade. At its detonation, they rushed the cabin. She maintained the veil despite knowing it would be less effective with such quick motion.

They reached the window without opposition. A glance inside revealed two men sitting next to an utterly unconcerned hostage who held a cigar in one hand and a coffee mug in the other. All of them wore goggles. The captors held pistols aimed at their hostage.

She cast a shield around the hostage as Angel smashed the window with his rifle butt. One man twisted toward the sound, firing paintballs at them blindly. The other kept his weapon pointed at the captive and pulled the trigger. Angel took the first down with a triple shot, then the second. He announced, "Clear."

After an interval in which they cleaned up and removed the most burdensome items of their gear, Cait and her unit were seated around a large rectangular table with the two hostage-takers and their captive, a current senator who was formerly a marshal and a friend of Elliott's. They'd shared some laugh-inducing stories with the rest of them about other tricks they'd pulled during their careers. Kingston asked, "So, you were in on it all along, boss?"

Elliott replied, "Nope. Joe put one over on me this time, too." He turned his head toward the senator and added, "Ya bastard."

Senator Rutter laughed. "Some things don't change, my friend." A coffee carafe and more mugs arrived, and Cait filled hers, dumping in a little sugar, something that, for some reason, she only did with her SOG colleagues.

Elliott said, "Today's action was an effective solution, but it might not have been in another case. Why is that, Lawson?"

Tori, codename "Brain" because of her frequently intimidating intellect, replied, "Anti-magic bullets."

The senator nodded and pointed his cigar at Cait. "Exactly."

She replied, "Absolutely. I wouldn't have made that same choice in a real hostage situation. I would've blasted everyone with lightning, including the hostage. The magic might have caused the guns to discharge, depending on how the opposition's nerves reacted to the electricity, but with enough surprise, I think it would've worked. Another option would have been to smash the bad guys away with force magic."

Julie frowned. "Has that electricity thing been tested?"

Cait replied, "Not that I'm aware of."

Tori added, "Nor I."

Elliott nodded. "We'll put it on the agenda for next time. Draw straws for who gets to be the unlucky ones holding the weapons."

Cait grinned. "I vote for Angel."

He smacked her on the arm. "Traitor." Then he said something in Spanish, a language that, around them at least, he only turned to when he wanted to insult them without their knowledge. When he finished, he added, "A couple of flash-bangs in front of the electrical attack might help."

Elliott nodded. "Tori, do the research. Find out what's known and what we need to figure out."

She replied, "Got it, boss."

An SUV pulled up outside the cabin, along the road they had pretended didn't exist during their scenario. Senator Rutter, Elliot, and the two hostage-takers climbed in, leaving the rest of the team to march back. Kingston shook his head at the departing vehicle with a laugh. "Typical. You'd think we were still in training." He turned to face her. "Can't you do your magic and float us to the base or something?"

From around her neck, Aza said, *"He seems smart."*

She laughed. "I could, but that would be cheating. I don't think any of us want to be running laps until nightfall." The reminder of that standard punishment from training drew a chorus of agreement that a comfortable hike through the forest was far preferable. She fell in line behind Tori, the leader when Elliott wasn't around, with Angel at her side. The camaraderie and closeness she felt when working with her team echoed the one she got at home in Ireland. *And the one I'll hopefully have soon in Boston.*

CHAPTER TWENTY-FIVE

The next morning, Cait finally had enough time to dig into the two criminal organizations in town. They were frequently referenced in the papers, along with their leaders, Leonard Rosetta and Yoshino Kyouka, although it was more often suspicions rather than verified acts they'd committed. At eleven, Clement walked past her desk and called, "Cait, just got word. The Dragons will meet with us. Come on."

She grabbed her suit coat from the back of her chair, tucked her paddle holster and Glock onto her belt, and hurried to catch up with him. They took the elevator to the basement and boarded the subway toward Chinatown. Cait asked, "Where's Garrett?"

He chuckled. "Busy doing something else on a different case. Besides, it wouldn't be fair for him to get all the luck that seems to come along with you. That discovery at the judge's house will get noticed."

She scowled. "If you call me a leprechaun, I'll cook your brain inside your skull."

He looked uncertain but mostly disbelieving as he asked, "You can do that?"

She laughed. "Nah. But it sounds good, doesn't it?"

"I was thinking more four-leaf clover than a leprechaun, anyway."

"You suck."

The walk through the streets of Chinatown was illuminating. Restaurants were everywhere, and where there wasn't a restaurant, the space seemed to be filled by nightclubs that hadn't yet opened for the day. The signage was bright, sometimes elegant, other times garish, but always eye-catching. They walked past a hospital, which offered a strange mix of the new and technological against the rest of the district's more old-world vibe.

Clement stopped at a dumpling shop, opening the door for her to enter. The inside was painted in cheerful yellow and black, calling sunflowers to mind, and held a dozen square tables and a long bar along one wall.

Two seats at the bar came open as they arrived, and they stepped past the departing diners to claim them. A female server behind the bar quickly cleared the previous occupants' debris away and slipped utensils and mats in front of them. They ordered dumplings, hers shrimp and his pork, which arrived with various dipping sauces and chopsticks that felt like they were indeed ivory.

The first bite was so good that she almost fell off her chair. She must have made a sound because Clement laughed. "I know. That was my first reaction, too. Their soup is equally amazing. Everything here is. This is my favorite restaurant in the district and one of the top ones in the city as far as I'm concerned."

She busied herself eating a couple more from the steamer tray, then asked quietly, "So, is this Dragon central?"

He patted his lips with the napkin and replied, "All of Chinatown is. The principal people in the organization move around, remaining visible and staying very obviously connected to the community. It's a much more hands-on approach than the Roses take."

To Cait, it seemed like a more effective one, too. "What do Rosetta's folks do?"

He let out a small laugh. "Assume everything is going well until it isn't, then bring baseball bats and guns to finish the problem in a way that sends a message to anyone else who might not live up to expectations."

She blinked. "Yikes. Remind me to ally with the Dragons if I ever decide to play for the other team."

He shook his head, and his voice lowered a little more. "Maybe not. They use *swords* and guns, and also tend toward early and decisive intervention."

She clicked her chopsticks against the dipping bowl. "Best to stay a marshal then, I guess."

He nodded, turning back to his food. "Yep."

Cait sighed. "There goes my retirement plan."

When they finished their meal, the server made eye contact with Clement and shifted her gaze toward a side hallway. He tapped Cait's elbow. "Here we go." She was two steps behind him as he walked down the passage. As they approached, a closed door at the end was opened by a man dressed in a black suit with a black shirt and tie and shiny black shoes. Even his pocket square was black. *I'm sensing a theme.*

He gestured for them to go up the stairs, and when they reached the top, a pair of men in identical outfits waited. They declared their guns and declined to give them up, citing regs when the men growled for them to hand them over, and underwent thorough and efficient if not particularly respectful pat-downs. One of the pair escorted them into an antechamber that held two more men in suits, these with pistols naked in their hands, then through a red lacquered panel door.

The room they entered was, in a word, gorgeous. It had a crimson couch to the left, along with a gold metal and glass coffee table. To the right was a trio of black leather chairs—large, luxurious wingback models.

The rug was filled with color and offered a nautical theme with waves, ships, and sea creatures. It ran to the elegant wooden desk at the far end, which had two more leather chairs in front of it, these a deep red. A woman sat behind its highly polished surface.

She wore a beautiful silk robe with a modern blouse visible where it parted when she moved. Her face was long and thin, with straight black hair pulled severely back. The only makeup she wore was on her eyes and lips, but both were dramatic and attention-grabbing.

Their escort gestured at the seats. "Madam, this is Deputy US Marshall Clement Austin, who we have met before. His companion is Deputy US Marshal Cait Keane, who we have not."

Her partner had remained standing, so Cait did the same. After a moment, the woman gave a small nod. "Please, be seated." Her words held more than a touch of a British accent, suggesting she'd learned English somewhere other than the States. "What can a humble restaurant owner do for the US Marshals?"

Clement replied, "With all due respect, madam, you are somewhat more than that."

The woman inclined her head. Cait pulled out her phone slowly and called up an image of the markings. "We are investigating the killing of Judge Meyer. His killer carved these into his back. We hoped you might be able to offer us some insight."

She held up her phone, and the black-suited man swept in and snatched it from her hand. He examined it carefully, front and back, removed the protective case, and checked that too. When he was satisfied, he positioned it so his boss could look at it. After staring at it for several seconds, Yoshino turned her face to them. "You believe this has to do with us?"

The man returned Cait's phone as Clement said, "Or maybe someone simply wants it to look that way. We are not in a position to draw conclusions yet since we're still gathering information. Given your connections throughout the city, we thought you might have heard something that could shed some light on it."

She steepled her fingers before her. Long scarlet nails and jeweled gold rings adorned them. "I know nothing of the killing except to say that none of mine was involved. This man Meyer. It is well-known that his courtroom was for sale to the highest bidder. Judge and jury both."

She offered a thin smile. "Perhaps that gives you a place to start. Also, in the future, perhaps do not make insinuations of guilt before you have actual evidence to support them."

Cait nodded automatically and followed Clement's lead as he rose. He said, "Thank you, madam."

The man in black gestured, and they headed for the exit. Before they reached it, the woman's voice carried to them. "Welcome to Boston, Deputy Marshal Keane. I hope our paths cross again under more pleasant circumstances."

She turned back and gave the woman a small bow. "Thank you, madam. I look forward to it."

They retrieved their weapons in silence and headed out of the restaurant without speaking. Once they were on the street, she asked, "What the hell was that?"

Clement laughed, but the sound held the frustration of a departure carrying more questions than they'd arrived with. "Maybe she wants to help with your retirement plans."

CHAPTER TWENTY-SIX

Cait was sitting at her desk paging through mugshots of people known to be associated with the Roses when Chief Levitt stuck his head out of his office. "Keane, a word?"

"Sure, boss." She locked down her computer and walked toward the chief's space, waving a rude gesture at Clement when he whispered, "You're in trouble."

She closed the door behind her and sat in one of the comfortable guest chairs across the desk from her superior. His office was spartan and functional, with only the desk, the two chairs in front of it, and a short couch along one wall. A metal bookcase stood behind him, filled with books and framed certificates. He asked, "How's it going?"

She laughed. "Good, real good. Can't say I expected, well, most of what's happened the last couple of weeks, but you know, we're Marshals. We adapt."

"True. So, what's on your desk?"

She replied, "Everything's more or less closed at the moment except the judge, the Roses, and the Dragons. You know. Little stuff." They shared a laugh. "What's up with the criminal organizations, anyway? Certainly they're too big to fly under the radar."

He sat forward in his chair again, set the mug on his desk, and paused, staring up. Finally, he said, "The best way to think of the organizations is that they're vicious dogs prowling outside the fence. As long as you don't interact with them, the status quo remains. They circle each other, maybe snap and growl here and there, but as long as we stay on our side of the fence and keep the gate closed, all is well."

"And if we cross the boundary?"

"Chaos reigns." His expression told her he wasn't kidding.

Cait crossed her arms. "That's okay with everyone, is it?"

"No," he snapped. "It's not." His voice softened. "Unfortunately, despite efforts by a lot of people in town, us included, the institutional will to do what it takes to eliminate the problem is lacking at the highest levels. So, we do what we can."

She let her arms fall, pushing her frustration aside. "Which is?"

Simon shrugged. "Interfere whenever we have cause and cover to do so."

"Like killing a judge."

"Just so. So, go find a way to interfere."

She closed the office door quietly behind her. Her awesome marshal skills immediately drew her attention to where Garrett and Clement stood around Sabrina's desk, which wasn't a common occurrence. She wandered over. "Is this a private party, or can anyone join?"

They made room for her, and Garrett explained, "Sabrina's doing her magic. Well, not her actual magic, only her run-of-the-mill, incredibly skilled work."

The other woman said, "Judge Meyer's money trail has led us somewhere."

Excitement twitched in Cait's stomach like butterflies. "Share."

The infomancer leaned back in her chair so she could look up at all of them at once. "Turns out we're not the only ones that hacked into that Caymans account."

Not what I was expecting. "Okay."

Sabrina nodded. "It's weird, right? Records show a large withdrawal the afternoon the judge died." She stopped talking, but the small smile on her lips suggested there was more to share.

Clement demanded, "Go on, tell us the rest."

"Seven hundred and seventy-seven thousand, seven hundred and seventy-seven dollars, and seventy-seven cents."

The numbers made no sense to Cait, but Clement breathed, "You're kidding."

Sabrina raised an eyebrow. "Nope."

Garrett said, "It could be a fake."

Cait asked, feeling as if she was missing something obvious, "What could be a fake?"

The infomancer explained, "That number is the calling card of the Syndicate."

Garrett shook his head. "Or someone wants us to *believe* it's the Syndicate."

Cait frowned. "Pretend like I haven't been in Boston very long, and I don't know what the hell you people are talking about."

Sabrina laughed. "It's not a Boston thing, but it isn't talked about too much in professional circles."

Garrett added, "By anyone other than conspiracy theorists, she means."

Clement explained, "Rumors say the Syndicate is an organization of assassins for hire. Some think they're simply a connection company to put people in touch with killers. Kind of like a dating service for murder. Others think they train and hire out their people to do the wet work."

Cait processed that information for a moment, then shoved it into a corner of her brain to worry about later. "So, is the idea that whoever hired one of them to kill the judge paid them off from the judge's account? That's cold."

Sabrina nodded. "Agreed, on both."

Cait said, "We're back to motive."

Clement shrugged. "Seems to me like the judge ticked somebody off in a big way, and they decided to take him out."

Cait asked, "Baseball bats or swords?"

"That's the question, isn't it?"

Sabrina said, "It still doesn't explain those symbols."

Garrett stretched, raising his arms toward the ceiling. "So, where do we go from here?"

Clement replied, "Let's spend some time researching the Syndicate. I'll get the chief to spring for dinner so we can put our heads together afterward if everyone's willing." For the reward of a free meal, they all were. When the business day ended, they walked several blocks to a different bar, one that didn't appear to have a substantial law enforcement presence inside. Instead, it was full of people who looked like bankers or young executives.

They claimed a table, ordered a round of drinks, and requested the house specialty, lobster macaroni and cheese. When they'd settled, Garrett said, "Okay. I'll start. I found out that the folks on the federal discussion boards I have access to don't think the Syndicate exists."

Clement replied, "I hit up some military intelligence contacts. They do believe it exists, but not as what it purports to be."

Sabrina let out a small snort. "You realize that didn't make any sense, right?"

Clement laughed. "What I mean to say is that they think it's a front. A myth to cover other things."

Cait sighed. "I came up dry, too. Did a search of newspapers and other media, found lots of rumors, but nothing substantial."

The food arrived, and they each took a moment to enjoy a few bites. Sabrina said, "Looks like I've got the best information of the bunch, which I think means I get at least one bite of each of your meals. Turns out groups exist on the magical dark web that claim to track Syndicate operatives."

Clement corrected, "Assassins."

Sabrina pointed her fork at him. "They call themselves operatives, supposedly."

Garrett asked, "Why?"

Cait replied, "Maybe they do things other than knock people off?"

Clement tapped the table with a finger. "Stay on topic, people." Their attention turned back to Sabrina, who said, "I reached out to a tracker. She believes one of the assassins came to town a few weeks ago, using the identity Carl Winston."

Cait replied, "Holy hell. A name?"

Garrett said, in a voice that was excited but tempered with restraint, "There must be dozens of people by that name in Boston. It's not exactly unique."

Sabrina nodded. "Eighteen once you consider that Carl could be spelled with a C or a K. According to the NSA, only one of them has a cell phone signal that's been moving from hotel to hotel every two days since a week before someone killed the judge."

CHAPTER TWENTY-SEVEN

When Cait came into work the next day, earlier than the rest of the office for once, she heard sounds coming from behind the door to Sabrina's dungeon. *Guess I'm not the first one in after all.* She knocked, and the infomancer called, "Come in." The woman swiveled in her seat as Cait entered. She looked like she was somewhere between exhausted and asleep in her chair, with dark circles under her eyes and a strange slackness to her features. Cait asked, "Are you okay?"

Sabrina laughed darkly. "This is why I have the couch, see? I can do the long hours when needed. I just have to pay the toll for them pretty quickly afterward. I'm fine. My challenges all have processes to deal with them."

Another knock sounded, and Sabrina called to allow them entrance. Clement and Garrett crowded in. The latter asked, "What you got?"

The infomancer swiveled back to face her computer and called up a new image on the large display. "The yellow marks are where we know our target has been, based on hotel system information and his cell phone intercepts."

Cait interrupted, "How did you get the NSA to play nice?"

Sabrina twisted around and smiled. "Infomancers aren't all about the traditional methods others use." She faced her monitors again. "So, working from that data, I've run an algorithm to create boundaries for where he's most likely to turn up next." An area of the map without a particular shape took on shading in light red. "I've been cracking into the hotels within those lines all night long. Surprisingly, some of the bigger ones have pretty solid security. I've got a half-dozen more to do."

Clement said, "Anything else we should know?"

Sabrina shook her head. "No, sorry. That's all the information I have."

He grinned. "You're awesome. Keep up the great work and let me know when you find something." He turned to them. "Let's give her some quiet to work in, huh?"

An hour later, Cait was listless and unable to concentrate. She'd already cleared her email inbox, straightened the papers on her desk, and cleaned off a coffee stain on its surface that had probably been deposited before her birth. Familiarizing herself further with fugitives and the city was always an option, but her lack of mental fortitude suggested it wouldn't be productive. She muttered, "Bored."

Aza replied, *"Only boring people get bored."*

With a whispered, "Shut it, you," she decided it was time to visit the evidence room. She hadn't seen it yet, since the tour postponed by the fugitive spotting on her first day had never materialized. Her research on the Roses and Dragons had also hit a dead end, and it was always possible that something down there might give her a useful lead. *It's a long shot, but sometimes the crazy bets pay off.*

She took the elevator down to the basement area above the subway, using her ID to convince the security in the lift that she had the authority to stop there. It took her credentials plus a ten-digit code to get into the spacious evidence corral. Unlike the one in Columbus, which had resembled an old, dusty library surrounded by prison bars in need of a paint job, this room radiated technology and sterility. As she stepped in from the hallway, a pleasant female voice said, "Welcome, Deputy Marshal Keane."

A visual survey of the area showed camera domes mounted every few feet on the ceiling, and she guessed that the speakers carrying the words were in there as well. "Hiya." The small area around her was rectangular, about six feet by ten, and served as an airlock to the room, doubtless for security and preservation purposes. She noted the presence of advanced fire suppression systems all around and felt the chill of a carefully controlled atmosphere.

The room asked, "How may I assist you?"

She replied, "I'm looking for materials from any cases involving the Roses or the Dragons."

The voice said, "Please stand by." A moment later, the door in front of her slid aside with a release of pressure that ruffled her hair. Several white tiles on the floor illuminated, displaying a path into the rows and rows of lockers beyond. "Please follow the markings. If you have any additional needs, you have only to speak your request."

"Thanks." She stepped through. The door slid closed

behind her, and she spared a moment to examine her surroundings more carefully. The evidence lockup resembled physical library stacks from an age gone by. That was the only similarity this room had to the one in Columbus. Everything here was white, and technology was a fundamental part of its design.

The storage lockers had no locks nor any clear mechanism to open them. The units were modular, each large section containing an identical set of lockers, ranging from the size of a safe deposit box to ones spacious enough to handle stacked file boxes taller than she was. Each locker held only a barcode for identification. She walked along the indicated path, and as she stepped off one square and onto the next, the one behind dimmed back to normal.

Cait turned left, walked a little way forward, then turned right. On the right-hand side, a short distance away, a tall locker door was slightly ajar, and the tile in front of it glowed a pale, comforting blue.

She opened it the rest of the way, discovering a small electronic display on the inside of the door listing the case details and the items contained within. She touched the case name, and the screen shifted to show a summary of the record. The items inside belonged to a case where a member of the Roses had allegedly gotten into a violent altercation with one of the Dragons.

The locker held a baseball bat, which inspired a dark inward chuckle, and a pair of pistols in transparent boxes. Each had a barcode associated with it. She pushed the door closed and continued along the lighted path. By the time she'd looked inside a dozen and only covered a tiny part of the vast space, she knew that her needle-in-a-haystack search was useless. She muttered, "Too much garbage, not enough data."

Aza replied in her mind, *"Perhaps a walk?"* Even in his jewelry form, he was happiest when he was outdoors.

"I don't have a better idea." She wandered outside, soaking in the comfort of being out in the sun and light breeze until her phone *pinged* to summon her back inside. Clement and Garrett were already present when she walked through the open door into Sabrina's workspace.

The infomancer said, "So, it looks like a dead end. He's no longer in town or no longer using that identity and phone. No sign of anyone who might be him in the hotels either, at least none my bots could find in the data. Although, with a little disguise or some assistance, he could still be staying at any of them."

Her tone conveyed her doubt.

Cait said, "But you don't think so."

The infomancer shook her head, making her dark ponytail swing from side to side. "No. I'm guessing one of two things happened. Either he allowed himself to be noticed in his earlier movements so we'd draw false conclusions, or he's gone quiet before another operation. And, to be clear, I'm using 'he' generically. It doesn't have to be a man."

Clement asked, "If you had to bet?"

Sabrina shrugged. "He's got something else planned. Seven hundred thousand and change seems like a lot for one judge."

They left the infomancer to rest and gathered in the office's conference room. Clement said, "All right. We've got a dead judge who was almost certainly up to nefarious things."

Garrett interrupted, "Unless he was a bird watcher."

"Granted. Also, we've got a potential assassin who whacked him, leaving strange characters carved in his flesh that seem to point to the Dragons."

Simon joined them. "Which means it couldn't have been the Dragons. Too obvious."

Cait replied, "Unless it's a double-blind. Make it seem too obvious, so we'll dismiss it out of hand."

Clement declared, "I think it's time we went out and pushed on some of these scumbags. See if we can shake something loose."

Garrett nodded, and Cait replied, "I'm in."

Simon said, "You have my blessing."

Clement laughed. "Gee, thanks, Chief."

Ten minutes later, she was in the passenger seat of Clement's Charger as they barreled through the streets of Boston. She said, "So, the target Sabrina gave us is a street soldier for the Dragons with an outstanding arrest warrant. He's been spotted, but no one swooped in to pick him up because he's a tiny fish."

Clement grunted. "Let's hope he gives us a bigger one once we've got him on the line." He cursed and spun the wheel, dodging around an electric motorcycle weaving in and out of traffic.

Sabrina said over their earpieces, "I have a drone watching him. Two blocks ahead, in the alley to your right."

Clement double-parked the car a block away from the target and activated its hazard lights. He stayed on that street while she jogged down an alley to the next one over. They advanced in parallel for a block and entered from both sides of their target's alley simultaneously.

The Dragon enforcer spotted Clement first and turned to walk away, only to see her coming in the other direction. His expression showed that he was calculating the odds of making it past her, and she called, "Don't. We're only here to talk. If you make me chase you, you're going to jail after you get done in the emergency room."

He stopped, tension filling his figure, and they closed to quiet speaking distance, continuing to stand between him and an opportunity to dash out of the alley. The man, whose face was riddled with acne scars visible under a scraggly beard and mustache, snarled, "I don't have anything for you people. What do you want?"

Clement asked, "You hear about the judge getting knocked off?"

The criminal shook his head. "Nah, man. I don't care about stuff like that. I just watch the streets."

She exchanged glances with her partner, then said, "We're not stupid. Word has to have gotten around."

"Look. I don't care about any judge, living or dead, unless I'm standing in front of them." They questioned him for a while longer but came away empty. They were both surly by the time they returned to the car. Clement growled, "Guess we'll do some more tomorrow. I'm not hopeful. The Roses and the Dragons are pretty good at avoiding hiring people who talk."

Cait nodded. "We'll find someone. Tomorrow is good." *But tonight is better.*

CHAPTER TWENTY-EIGHT

Cait stood in the shadows of an alley across from the Casale Cheese Company. Aza was beside her, invisible thanks to his camouflage scales. She whispered, "We'll try here first since we know this is a Roses place. If we don't find anything, we'll head to Chinatown and see if we can identify one of the Dragons' hangouts or hideouts or whatever. Before you ask, no, we can't burn it down."

When she'd considered infiltrating the building, it had been in the abstract. Since she'd planned for it, there had been a lot more involved than she'd anticipated. In preparation for the night's adventure, she'd snagged a black watch cap from a box of winter clothes she hadn't unpacked yet and portaled to Louisiana to retrieve her black fatigues.

Then, feeling strangely suspicious, she'd added the equipment belt she'd brought back from her home village and the knives in her wrist sheathes. Finally, her pistol was holstered at her lower back, although if she had to use it, she'd probably wind up in some serious administrative trouble with the Marshals. It felt weird, this cross-pollination of her various selves, yet also somehow correct. *Maybe I should wear my blades every day, play it off like it's normal. Wonder how that would go over with the chief.*

With a snort, she checked her bracelet even though she knew it was right where it was supposed to be, above her sheath and against her skin so she could cast with it. She warned the dragon, "Here we go, Aza," and blasted force magic into the ground to carry her to the roof of the building next to them. From there, she launched herself over to the top of the large structure that housed the cheese company.

She whispered the spell to expand her senses and moved along the roof in a crouch, listening carefully for anything that would give her insight into what lay below. She wasn't carrying her cell phone or any of her marshal's electronic equipment, so there wouldn't be a record of her presence here. Tonight, she needed to have deniability since there was no way to know what might happen.

She finally heard voices when she reached the far end of the roof but couldn't make out what they were saying. Aza remarked from where he flew lazy circles above, *"Metal stairs on the side of the building to your right."* She turned and spotted the top posts of the fire escape and climbed over, descending to the first platform and the door it held. She muttered, "Damn, now I wish I'd brought some electronics." It was almost certain that the door would be alarmed, and she didn't have an easy way to defeat it.

Aza offered, *"I could provide a distraction."*

She grinned, shaking her head at his enthusiasm for destruction. "No, we want to be quiet, not start a fire."

"I can do other things than fire, you know."

"Like what?" She baited him.

He growled, *"I can bite people. Would you like a personal demonstration?"*

She laughed at his intentional ferocity. "No, but I believe you. One hundred percent. I don't suppose you've got anything to help with this alarm, though."

"Only a distraction."

She sighed. "We'll consider that our last resort. You know, there almost has to be some sort of access to the roof from inside. Do a flyover, see if you can find anything that looks like it might be a movable panel."

Cait climbed back to the roof. The dragon found the opening after a couple of passes, easily missed because it was in the middle of a square of HVAC equipment. She had to hold her breath and squeeze to make it through the gap between the devices but was able to enter the building through the unlocked cover. No alarms went off.

She stepped off the ladder onto a catwalk that criss-crossed the entire space under the ceiling, allowing for replacing overhead lights and access to the roof. Wrapping herself in a visual shield and adding a muffling spell to diminish the sound of her feet on metal, she made her way down the staircase toward an office on the third floor. This level ran along the building's outer skin, as did the one below it, offering a view down to the bottom.

On the ground floor, forklifts darted and whirred while people shouted, moving things to and fro as they loaded an eighteen-wheeler parked at the loading dock. She stayed low so a random upward glance wouldn't spot any shimmer of her visual shield. Aza, doubly hidden by her efforts and his scales, paced at her side. She'd been surprised when he'd flown in a second after her, his stature reduced so he could pass easily through the opening before she'd closed it. He was again in his normal small dog size, traveling along in front of her. His tail swayed back and forth as he moved in a way that made her think of a predator on the hunt. *Right now maybe that's exactly what he is.*

They crouched in a secluded area near an office, and she focused her full attention on it. Two men spoke to one another inside, clear to her powered-up hearing. One of them was the man who'd led them to the location previously, and she whispered, "Not Rosetta's voice. Probably the guy we followed is a middle person."

The men discussed mundane things, what was presumably ordinary business stuff for the cheese company, then one came out. He was dressed in cheap khakis and a white button-down with short sleeves and looked harried as he hustled down the stairs toward ground level. *Manager of the night shift, maybe. Doesn't look like he's got a fun job.*

The first man's voice resumed speaking, lower than it had been and filled with flirty entendre as he talked with someone, suggesting they meet up later. She whispered, "Wife, girlfriend, mistress. Whatever. We've got to get him before he calls for a car or something. Let's move."

Cait added a layer of force protection to the sight and sound muffling spell she was using, expanding it to include Aza. She pulled the watch cap down to cover her face, still able to see adequately enough through the tiny holes.

They moved in a crouch to the office door, and she turned the knob slowly, thoroughly pleased when it turned out not to be locked. She shoved it open and rushed through, the dragon at her side, and gently kicked it closed as soon as they were inside. The room was utilitarian with a thin carpet under standard office furniture, including a metal desk with a man in a fairly nice suit behind it.

He reached for a desk drawer, and she blasted him with lightning, holding it on him until he slumped in his chair, unconscious. She paused, listening carefully to see if anyone had noticed her actions. No yelling or footfalls materialized. "Okay. Let's get him ready for a chat."

When he showed the first signs of returning to consciousness, she gave him a hard slap across the face. His eyes popped open, and his body convulsed, his survival instincts prodding him to move, to fight or flee. Unfortunately for him, the electrical cords and computer cables she'd used to bind his arms and legs to the chair prevented both.

He shouted for help, and she shook her head. "No one can hear you." Her voice came out deeper, more gravelly than usual as part of the illusion she had summoned to hide her features. When he looked at her, he would see a dark blur, ghostly and ominous. When he stopped struggling, she nodded. "Hi there. We're going to ask you some questions."

The man growled, "We? I only see one of you, you freak."

"Oh, no. I'm not alone. Aza?"

The dragon was now the size of a Great Dane. He padded forward and let his scales shift back to visibility, offering their captive an image of him as a black beast with a red stripe from nose to tail. The man swore, and she laughed. "You may have noticed that we took off your shoes and socks. There's a reason for that." She looked down at her partner. "Want to show him?"

Aza continued moving forward. In her mind, he said, *"This is more like it."* He opened his mouth and breathed gently. Flames licked out, lightly caressing the gangster's feet. He screamed and struggled, but to no avail.

Cait said, "That's maybe a first-degree burn, but I bet it hurts like it's more. Burns always do. And, so you know, he likes his meat *very* well done."

The guy said, sweating and hurried, "Okay, tell me what you want. Damn. There's no need to get all uncivilized."

She replied, "Someone killed a federal judge. What do you know?"

He scowled. "Yeah, I know a lot about that. We've been on alert for the person that knocked him off. Word is the Dragons hired the killer because the judge took a payoff and failed to deliver.

"That would have probably been cause enough, but the reason he didn't come through is because we outbid them. So, they carved him up and took him out." The man shook his head. "They're animals over there. No bend in them at all. Don't understand business." He said the words like they deeply offended him.

"Okay, so you say he works for the Dragons. I guess I can see why that might concern Mr. Rosetta."

The man in the chair grunted. "Don't know this Rosetta you're talking about. But my boss has the word out to find the killer."

She rolled her eyes at the denial. "And?"

He sighed. "We've only been able to come up with a

name. Club Suyin. Supposedly, he hangs out there. It's in Chinatown if you haven't guessed that yet."

She thought maybe punching him in the face would feel good, given the attitude he was sending her way. The professional side of her resisted. During the pause, Aza gave him another light burst of flame. She rested her hand on his back, and he subsided.

Their captive spent almost a full minute writhing and swearing before he turned his attention back to her. She said, "I'm supposed to believe an assassin is hanging out at a club, enjoying Boston's nightlife?"

The man laughed with an edge of desperation. "I don't know. What's he going to do, hang out in a fleabag hotel somewhere? I guess even hired killers need some R&R now and again."

Cait scowled at him but didn't sense he had any further information to share. "All right. You get to stay uneaten for now. I think keeping an eye on Mr. Rosetta—oh, I mean your *boss*—would be a wise choice."

She called up a ball of lightning in her hand. "Oh, and if you let anyone know we talked, I'll find out, and we'll be back. If you think a little first-degree burn on your feet is bad, wait until you see how much it hurts right before you're cooked enough to eat." Before he could reply, she shocked him into unconsciousness again.

CHAPTER TWENTY-NINE

By the time they'd gotten the information about the club the night before, it had been too late for Cait to use it. So, after putting in a normal day of US Marshaling, during which she and Garrett braced several low-level workers from each of the criminal organizations with no appreciable results, she went shopping. When she returned to her hotel two hours later, she had everything she needed for the evening.

Aza looked at her quizzically as she came through the door with shopping bags in both hands. She shook her head, warned, "Don't ask," and headed for the shower.

She'd decided that the only viable option to find their target at the nightclub was to go in and search for him. And she couldn't do that as Cait Keane, US Marshal. So, she'd made some purchases to ensure she didn't look anything like her professional self.

First, she put dye in her hair, using two packages worth to make sure it was fully coated. With it piled on top of her head, she used the time while it did its work to page through maps of the location on her phone, memorizing potential escape routes should she get into trouble.

When the dye was complete, she went into the shower and washed her hair, blew it dry, and pulled it up in a pair of ponytails, one on each side of her head. Then, with a sigh of irritation, she opened a bottle of self-tanner and sprayed it carefully over her face and along her body from hips to head.

She dug into her shopping bags and dragged out a matching set of leather garments, pants and a bikini top. She put both on, then dropped a very low-cut electric blue blouse over them. Her tattoos were on display, which would help since as far as she knew, no one local was aware that Cait Keane, US Marshal, had them.

She'd purchased a second blouse, identical to the first, and cut out pieces of cloth to wrap around her wrists to hide her bracelet. Low black boots went on next, showing a small slit of skin between them and her pantlegs.

She put sticky metal studs on her nose and above her lip, where they looked exactly like piercings. Finally, she applied fake nails and painted them a brilliant yellow. Once it was complete, she peered at the mirror and shook her head. The woman staring back was different and didn't fit her image of herself at all. "Now I remember why I prefer pubs. Jeans and a t-shirt, good to go."

From his position on the bed where he'd watched her preparations, Aza asked, *"Is this a mating ritual?"*

She turned to face him. "Kind of, I guess."

He tilted his head to the side. *"Isn't it usually the males who try to impress?"*

She pointed at him. "And that's exactly what's wrong with people, right there, my friend." She shoved some cash into her pocket and slipped her phone into her waistband. "Okay, let's do this."

She summoned a car, and the dragon flew above it. Once they arrived in Chinatown, she walked from a couple of streets away to get in line at the club so no one could connect the car to her. She whispered into the phone she held to her ear as a disguise, "So, I wonder if that guy was right about the Dragons being involved."

From his perch on a nearby building, invisible to most but noticeable to her because she knew where to look, he observed, *"I don't like that they use that name."*

She chuckled. "Understandable."

He sounded worried as he said, *"I won't be able to watch you when you go inside."*

It made something in her chest feel warm to know he was concerned for her. "That's okay. I can take care of myself. If there's trouble, I promise I'll make it a point to get outside where you can help."

"Or scream my name. If I hear it, I'll come to you."

Cait lowered her voice and whispered, "We need to be sure that no one who doesn't deserve it gets hurt, bud. That's an absolute rule."

"Yes," he answered, but his tone didn't convince her he was completely committed to the notion.

After twenty minutes, she finally gained admittance to the packed club. The security inside gave her a once-over but apparently decided her outfit provided nowhere for her to hide anything dangerous and didn't interfere with her as she moved toward the bar. That was a definite downside to the costume—she couldn't hide a weapon anywhere in the tight pants, and her stylish boots weren't amenable to smuggling anything in, either. She'd chosen not to carry a purse to keep her hands free.

Cait ordered a piña colada, then pretended to sip from the tall, narrow glass as she moved around the crowded first level. The club throbbed with loud music, heavy bass and a relatively slow beat, sexy instead of frenetic. The dance floor was packed, bodies smashed together like one massive hunk of flesh rather than individual components. Fog swirled, lights flashed and danced, and occasionally confetti rained down.

When she glanced up to find its source, she ran her eyes across the second and third levels, which held tables that circled the outside so anyone sitting at them could watch the people below. Hanging from the ceiling at various heights were giant golden birdcages with scantily clad female dancers inside them. *We're not in Ohio anymore, Dorothy.*

She climbed the stairs to the second level, thinking that if she was to choose the most defensible position in the place, that's where she would be. She stood along the railing at the top of the steps, making a point of looking down at the people below, but flicked her eyes up and around to examine each table in turn, slowly and methodically. Her gaze crossed over the parts of the third floor she could see from her current angle.

She was halfway through before she spotted him. A man with dark hair and dark eyes, clean-shaven, skin tanned like he'd been out in the sun. He sat at a table with two women, his arms around the backs of their chairs, and looked for all the world as if he was simply a normal guy out for a night on the town.

She saw the truth in his eyes: the hardness, the cold calculation, the subtle wariness that kept him from fully engaging in the hedonism around him. Inside, she knew he was the one she was looking for. *Carl Winston, I presume.*

It took her a moment to realize her eyes had stopped scanning, and that he was staring back at her equally hard. He lifted an eyebrow, then rose from his seat. She moved along the second level, gently moving servers out of her way and growling at the people who packed the narrow aisle. She lost sight of him, found him again, headed toward the rear of the building, then he passed out of view once more. When she got to where she'd last spotted him, he was gone. The two women were looking in her direction, but she decided it was useless to ask them anything.

With a loud snap, the lighting truss suspended over the dance floor swung wildly, one of its support chains broken. She heard a door slam behind her as she spun and cast a line of force at the metal structure to keep it from falling, not sure if it would have done so if she hadn't acted. A moment later, other magicals in the crowd had it under control, and she dashed for whatever exit he'd taken.

In her mind, Aza said, *"Running man from the second floor."*

She broke outside and called, "Don't lose him."

The dragon replied, *"Got it."*

She was on yet another fire escape and whispered a quiet word of appreciation for Boston's adherence to construction codes. She ran up the metal stairs, gaining the roof a dozen seconds later. The dragon flew in the distance, visible thanks to the bright scales along his back that reflected the moonlight.

Cait blasted the roof with force magic, sending herself flying toward the next one, where she landed, tumbled into a roll to absorb her velocity, and came up running. She repeated the process at the next cross street, then again at the junction between buildings, not comfortable relying only on her physical skills at her current speed.

Aza kept up an ongoing monologue in her mind, telling her which way their quarry turned, and where the dragon thought he was heading. He said, *"He's walking now. I could get him if these people moved."*

She panted, "We don't want him dead. We need to know who hired him."

The dragon growled with evident dissatisfaction. *"He's in an alley."* She launched herself over the street, landing on a building below the hovering dragon. Aza clarified, *"Now he's inside."*

She ran over to the edge and looked down the alley, spotting the door he must have gone through. She put her hands on her thighs and drew several deep breaths, bringing her mind and body under control. "Okay. We're too close to let the bastard escape. See if you can find another way in, maybe from above. Once I get inside, I'll let you know if we can go loud."

"Got it." He sped away from her position.

She leapt down into the alley, using force magic to cushion her landing. Putting an ear to the door, she heard nothing from within. "Okay, here goes." She turned the handle but found it locked. Grumbling, she channeled fire magic into her hand and set it against the join of frame and door until they deformed enough that she could yank it open. She stepped inside into the darkness.

CHAPTER THIRTY

As soon as she passed through the door into the lightless building, Cait was on the defensive. The scrape of a foot was her only warning, and she ducked and slid aside as her low-heeled boots slipped on the uneven surface beneath her. She couldn't see her enemy but heard the *whish* of a weapon passing above her. She instinctively shouted and threw a wide wave of force magic toward where she thought the attacker was and barked "Tintreach" to create a hovering ball of electricity over her head.

It manifested in time for her to see the man she'd blasted slam into a table near a wall, landing on it and tumbling over, the furniture following him to the floor. Her mind categorized the scene in front of her impassively as her heart rate increased. She summoned more balls of light and threw them into the air, then covered herself in a skin of force magic.

The room looked like a restaurant but with blackened furniture, soot-covered walls, and water damage. *So, a fire not repaired.*

Eight people were inside, which seemed like a lot only for her. One was down, but the others were advancing, each holding an improvised weapon. A piece of wood here, a metal section torn from a chair there. One of them had a heavy frying pan. *They want deniability.*

At the end of the dining room to her left lay a pass-through to the kitchen, so the diners could see the chefs at work. One person stood between her and it, and she realized it was the only place of safety she'd find in the building, however temporary. She ran at the man, blasting him with a burst of force magic aimed at his feet that knocked them out beneath him and dropped him face-first onto the floor.

She stomped on him in passing and launched herself into the air to dive through the opening into the kitchen. Bullets followed her, and she realized she hadn't noticed guns were present. *Not good, Cait.* Her internal voice, not being a jerk for once, suggested that maybe they had been hiding them, which was a legitimate possibility.

She used her telekinesis to grab a heavy refrigerator, slid it in front of the door, and crouched behind it, ready to blast anyone who might come in the same way she had. *Stupid outfit. I should've brought a gun.* Sounds came from the other room, quick bursts of hushed conversation. She laughed inwardly. *Oh, so you're planning something clever, are you? Well, I've got an answer for that.* She shouted, "Aza, now."

He'd been flying furious loops around the building, looking for the best way in. He didn't know when Cait wanted him to join the fight and was reluctant to speak into her mind for fear of distracting her when she was in danger. His life had been simple when he was with the dragons, free of the uncertainty he now faced. Then she had appeared, and he'd felt pulled to her, knowing they were destined to be together. *We still have some things to work out.*

Then she shouted, and everything became clear. He knew where she was in the restaurant through his connection to her and had determined the weakest point in the ceiling while he waited. Since those two were not in the same place, his path was obvious. He flapped his wings, flying up for two seconds, then reversed and threw himself down at the roof, beating his wings to gain speed.

He curled into a ball as he struck, ensuring his scales took the full impact as he broke through, then unfolded and landed with a roar as debris rained down around him. Half of the enemies ran at the sight of him, heading toward the area where his partner was. He roared, ready to blast them with flames, when she called, "No fire. This place will cave in."

With a growled, *"Fine,"* he spun quickly, lashing his tail out at the enemy. It smacked into the nearest man, propelling him into the one beside him. They both flew away as he finished the spin and whipped out a clawed paw to rake at the next closest. That man managed to get the heavy stick he held in front of the blow, but it didn't impede Aza's claws. Flesh and wood shredded, and his foe fell with a howl of pain.

He dashed forward at the remaining untouched enemy, lowering his head at the last moment and sending him flying from the impact. One of the first pair had returned, announcing his arrival with a strike from the metal bar he held. It chimed a little as it struck his scales but otherwise had no effect.

Aza looked at him with a baleful eye, growled, *"Idiot,"* and drew in a breath to blast him. Then, remembering, he snorted out the air and smiled at his enemy. The man turned, dropped his weapon, and ran for the door.

The first person to come over the counter took a force blast to the face, spinning him into the far wall and removing him from the fight. Cait retreated from the others, who fired as they entered, and used the partially warped metal kitchen furniture to protect her from their rounds. *Probably not anti-magic, but it would be stupid to trust that guess.*

She reached up and quietly took two pans from a hanging rack along the wall. As bullets whined around her position, she muttered, "Not quietly enough, apparently." When the gunfire paused, she stepped out, barked, "Hey, scumbags," and threw both pans with all her strength.

The one from her right hand flew true, and she used her magic to nudge the other into an appropriate line. They struck her opponents almost simultaneously, knocking them down. She ran to them and delivered a punch to their heads, ensuring they'd stay out. She called, "Aza, we clear?"

He replied, "Yes. It's safe out here." She climbed over the counter and shook her head at the damage the dragon had done to furniture and foes alike. She laughed. "You're not subtle, you know?"

He grinned. *"Of course not. I'm a dragon."*

"That's your answer for everything, is it?"

"Maybe."

She said, "I'm not sure if this was only a backup option or if the ambush was the objective. Either way, our assassin has to be somewhere nearby. He'd want to see the results firsthand, so he'd know if he was still in danger."

Aza's head bobbed. *"Agreed."*

"Okay, here's the plan." A moment later, she watched as the dragon crouched, then launched himself back up through the hole he'd created in the ceiling, flapping his wings with fast strokes that buffeted her with their breeze. He was deliberately not camouflaged, the better to attract the assassin's attention. A few seconds after leaving the building, he sent into her mind, *"I've got him. Two buildings away."*

"Good. Keep him distracted."

The dragon replied, *"With pleasure."*

She used force magic to send herself up to the roof through the same opening, landed cleanly, then hopped quickly away as the surface creaked under her feet. She looked toward where Aza was cutting through the air a few buildings away and spotted the figure on the roof beneath, his back facing her. *Perfect, buddy.*

A blast of force sent her flying in a high arc that would carry her onto the same rooftop as her quarry. She landed and skidded, the fashionable footwear failing her again. She muttered, "Stupid boots."

The man had turned to face her at the sound of her arrival. Cait gave him a nod. "US Marshals. You're under arrest. Drop your weapons and lie on your face with your hands behind your back."

He laughed. "Now, what fun would that be?"

CHAPTER THIRTY-ONE

Cait glared at the laughing assassin. He continued, "You survived the trap. Well done. Bought you a few extra minutes of life."

Aza landed beside her, furled his wings, and let out a loud snarl. *"Want me to burn him?"*

She said quietly, "Let's keep that in reserve for now. I'd like him to be able to answer questions. How good is your control?"

He replied, "Maybe not perfect."

She nodded, her eyes never leaving the assassin, who had taken a step back at the dragon's arrival. "If you get an opening to hit him in a way you're sure won't kill him, take it. Otherwise, leave him to me." She moved away from the dragon, and he mirrored her.

Their foe kept backing up, reached around to his back with his left hand, and pulled out a large blade. Silver glinted with reflections of nearby neon as he twirled the dagger. He said, "If you both leave now, no one has to die tonight."

Cait replied, "If you surrender now, you can avoid potentially permanent debilitating damage."

He laughed. "That's some banter you've got there, Marshal. Are you new at this?"

She scowled and advanced at him. He whipped his right hand suddenly forward, and a barrage of sharpened ice stakes appeared in the air. Half of them headed for her. The rest angled toward Aza. She summoned a fire shield to intercept them, and the dragon simply dropped and rolled to avoid his. She growled, "Yes, our theory of a magical killer holds up."

Aza replied, *"Always nice to be right."*

"I wouldn't have minded being wrong on that one." *Of course, then we'd be fighting two rather than one, probably, so maybe not.* He tried the icicles again, but her defenses were adequate, and she continued to close.

His right hand darted behind his back again and came out with a pistol. She summoned a second shield of force magic to protect her as she turned to run on the assumption he'd loaded with anti-magic rounds. Bullets slammed into the roof beside and ahead of her, narrowly missing, and she skidded behind the building's chimney. More rounds impacted the brickwork, sending chips flying.

She risked a look around the corner of her cover to see that the man had drawn a second gun in place of the knife and was firing at the dragon. "Aza, look out." She had a moment of unwilling appreciation for how his arms seemed to work independently, the one continuing to send rounds at her, still on target as his eyes and other gun tracked the dragon.

Aza rolled into a ball, tucking his head and legs in. He

reminded her of an armadillo dropping into a defensive position. When the bullets hit him, she gasped, but they ricocheted rather than penetrating. She called, "Are you okay?"

The dragon laughed in her head. *"Takes more than that to get through my scales."*

"You're something, buddy. Let's get those guns out of play."

When the gunfire slackened, and her mental count suggested he probably needed to reload, she stepped out from cover. She reached out with her telekinesis, grabbed the right-hand gun, and ripped it from his grip, hurling it onto a different rooftop. Simultaneously, Aza unrolled, leapt into the air, and whipped around, his tail smacking the second pistol away.

Cait walked deliberately forward, using her magic to create a fighting stick out of magical force that very much resembled her favorite shillelagh. Holding it in her right hand, she pulled out her phone with the left and hit the emergency call button, then shoved it back in her pocket. While she did so, the assassin produced his knife again and a second one that matched it.

She called to Aza, "If I lose, he's all yours." Then she stopped walking and shifted into a fighting position. "You're done, dude. Pack it in. If I don't get you, my friend will."

He shrugged and replied, "The rules of my organization don't allow failure, Marshal."

"So, the Syndicate is real, huh?"

He gave her a wry smile. "I'm sure I don't know what you're talking about."

Cait sighed. "Right."

He gestured with the dagger. "Last chance. You could leave. Live to fight another day. I'm guessing you don't get paid enough to risk your life so easily."

She shrugged. "Danger comes with the territory. You could surrender."

He shook his head. "We appear to be at an impasse."

"Seems like."

He attacked, apparently out of pithy comments. He held his right knife reversed along his forearm, ready to slash on a forehand or backhand, his other blade held point forward, angled up. She twirled the shillelagh as he came in, then smacked the hard edge down against his left dagger as it stabbed at her throat. The blow carried his arm out to the side, opening him for a counter, but she had to lean back as the other blade passed in front of her face.

She knew he'd stab it back immediately and threw herself to the left, lunging out of its way. He moved in again and tried a low kick that she stopped with an upraised foot. She slammed it down at his knee in her kick, but he circled that limb back out of the way, spinning fast and coming in with a stab from his right-hand blade.

She met that attack force against force, slamming her shillelagh into his arm, aiming for his elbow. He extended enough that the blow struck him on the fleshy part of his upper arm. She growled at the missed opportunity as she pushed forward against him, trying to knock him off-balance. He stumbled toward the edge of the roof, and she had the perfect chance to hit him with a blast of magic. She restrained the impulse, wanting him alive to question later, not splattered on the ground three stories below.

The assassin charged in, feinting with the knives, and slammed a knee into her stomach. It drove the breath from her lungs momentarily, and she fell sideways into a half-roll, half-somersault to escape whatever follow-up might be coming next. As she propelled herself back to her feet, Aza flashed between them, cutting off his advance.

Her foe snarled, "You can't beat me one-on-one, huh?"

She coughed, getting her wind back. "I'm a little rusty. Moved to a new city, been neglecting my training. You know how it goes."

He scowled and resumed his attack, but the confident arrogance he'd displayed before was gone. They went back and forth, him slashing with the knives, her defending with her force club, and sneaking in counterstrikes when she could. He grew less precise and angrier as the fight continued.

Cait relaxed, gaining confidence with each pass. Her job in Columbus hadn't involved battling all that many magicals, and she realized being in that unexpected situation had made her nervous.

Now, the various pieces of her life were falling properly into place, creating a whole that was stronger than any of her separate roles. She changed up her footwork, moving with disguised intent, slipping away as he struck rather than meeting his force as she worked to position him where she wanted. When he was in place, she delayed until he committed to an attack, then dispelled her club and blasted him with force magic, sending him flying away from her to slam into the chimney.

His weapons flew from his hands as he struck, then the brickwork collapsed. He tipped over, falling backward. Aza darted into view, biting down on the assassin's lower leg and dragging him from the potential tumble down the shaft. Cait breathed, "Good job, buddy."

She walked over to the downed man, who was unconscious. She wrapped him in force magic, paying special attention to applying pressure above the deep punctures the dragon had put in his leg. A realization struck her, and she groaned. "Damn."

Aza crouched defensively. *"What?"*

She chuckled darkly. "I never thought about the fact that if things went well tonight, the other Marshals would see me in this outfit."

CHAPTER THIRTY-TWO

Cait arrived at the office late the next day, having been up until the wee hours getting her captive processed at the nearest lockup. No one paid attention to her entrance, but when she reached her desk, she found it covered in neon bracelets and glow necklaces like someone might wear to a rave. She laughed and called, "You guys suck."

Her colleagues materialized from hiding places around the room, laughing and offering a smattering of applause. Chief Levitt's door opened, and he said, "Keane, can I see you for a moment?"

She entered his office and sat across the desk from him. He pulled the stopper from a bottle of scotch, pouring a bit into each of two tumblers, and slid one to her. He capped the bottle again and raised his glass. "To success." She clinked glasses and drank the whisky. Then he grinned and added, "Congratulations on a successful capture."

She nodded. "Thanks, Chief."

"Now let's discuss what you did wrong." Cait winced as

Aza laughed in her head. Simon said, "You should have called for backup earlier."

She blinked when he didn't say anything more. "That's it?"

He shrugged. "Following leads is your job. I'm certainly not going to criticize you for that. How you do it is your choice, generally speaking. But sometimes, those choices will put you in danger. So, you shouldn't go it alone. That's asking for trouble."

"I see."

Simon chuckled. "I'm sure you don't. This sort of deep wisdom only comes with age and experience, and did I mention, age? The thing is, you're good, and this time you won. But it only takes one bad break to make things go wrong. When that happens, without backup, you're toast. Trust your colleagues."

She replied, somewhat defensively, "I do."

He nodded. "Then I'll assume you were being stupid on this one. Don't be stupid again. We'd like to keep you around for a while."

"Gotcha, boss."

His phone rang, and he waved her away. Aza said, *"You were never alone."*

Cait whispered, "Yeah, but I doubt it's the right time to share that."

"The guy we beat might mention me."

She hadn't considered that, and it caused her stride to falter. "Good point. I didn't think about that. Guess we'll have to hope no one takes him seriously."

She returned to her desk, and a moment later, Clement, Garrett, and Sabrina were looking down at her. Clement asked, "Did you get the 'trust your team' one or the 'no loose cannons' one?"

She laughed. "The former."

He grinned. "That's what passes for approval around here. Nice work. But really, call sooner."

She took in his serious expression, duplicated on the others' faces, and nodded. "You've got it."

Garrett changed the subject, "Your guy lawyered up."

Cait groaned. "Damn. Should have beaten some information out of him before we turned him over." Only part of her was joking.

He smiled. "You'll learn, grasshopper."

Sabrina asked, "Did you figure out who he was working for?"

Cait scowled. "Oh, I have a pretty good idea."

A couple of hours later, she rode up the tall elevator to the law offices of Sherman, Glass, and Burke, this time with Clement at her side. They encountered the same receptionist, were escorted by the same lawyer, and ditched their gear in the same locker room. Rosetta didn't rise at their entrance, nor did he attempt to take her hand. Today his suit was darker than before, but otherwise, he looked the same.

Cait lowered herself into her seat. "In case you haven't had the pleasure, this is Deputy US Marshal Austin."

Rosetta nodded. "Heard of you."

Clement smiled. "Hopefully good things."

Cait said, "As you requested last time, I wanted to make

you aware that someone in your organization must be untrustworthy."

Rosetta straightened. "That's good to know."

"I didn't put it together right away, but after a while, I realized that if the assassin had been working for the Dragons as you thought, he would've had more support in Chinatown." She kept her eyes locked on his expression, which didn't change in response to her words. *You're one cool criminal, Rosetta.*

She continued, "Seriously, he would at *least* have found a better ambush spot. So, the only logical conclusion is that he was working for you. I mean, your people." Rosetta began to speak, and Cait raised a hand to stop him. "I'm aware. It wasn't you, wasn't your organization. And the truth is, I can't prove it. Yet. But I thought you should know that I know. And that I take attempts to kill me kind of personally."

The lawyer attempted to intervene, but Rosetta shushed her. "That sounds like a threat, Marshal Keane."

She placed a palm on her chest as if shocked. "Absolutely not, Mr. Rosetta." She dropped the hand, and her voice hardened. "If I decide to threaten you, it won't be subtle, trust me." She stood and headed for the door, feeling Clement do the same.

Before she got there, she stopped and turned back. "Before I go, I have to ask. One of your men fed me the information that led me to the assassin and thus to the ambush. Do you think the intent all along was to kill me? Is that why the assassin was still in town?"

Rosetta shook his head, his lips pressed into a thin line. "I'm sure I don't know, Marshal."

She shrugged. "Well, lovely to see you again, Mr. Rosetta."

"Marshall Keane."

When they reached the privacy of the elevator, Aza said, *"That was brilliant. Do I get to burn him?"*

She snorted. "Maybe."

Clement asked, "What?"

Oops. "Maybe we should go take a run at our new friend Carl. Maybe he'll have something to say. Give us a lead we can use next time against Rosetta."

He checked his watch. "Sure. We've got time to kill before the thing."

She frowned. "What thing?"

Clement turned to her with a smile. "After your first successful case, you get a party at The Shillelagh, where we spend the evening pointing out your character flaws so you don't get a big head."

She laughed. "How long was yours?"

He sighed. "Beat the previous record by thirty-two minutes."

Cait grinned wide. "Amateur. Prepare to be dethroned."

THE STORY CONTINUES

Cait Keane and her Dragon partner Aza have a score to settle with an assassin – and whoever hired him. Everybody wants a word with the killer – the Marshals, the PDA, and the two criminal bosses in town. One of the bosses hired the hitman and he's not saying a word. Cait better slice through the tangle of lies fast. Continue her adventure in *WITCH WITH A GRUDGE*!

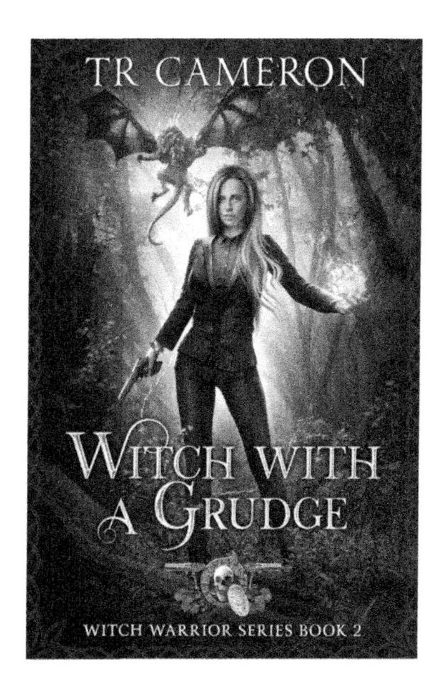

Claim your copy today!

AUTHOR NOTES - TR CAMERON

APRIL 4, 2022

Thank you for joining me on Cait's adventure! I hope you enjoyed reading the first book as much as I enjoyed creating it.

Important note: I've written a Cait short story for you to enjoy, about her earliest days with the Special Operations Group. You can find it here:.

https://dl.bookfunnel.com/19b0d79omx

It's yours for the minor commitment of signing up for my newsletter. I have absolutely no problem if you want to then unsubscribe from my newsletter. But with social media as quirky as it's been of late, I'd love to have a channel to communicate with you that I can depend upon.

As I write this, having turned in my manuscript yesterday, I'm a little worried. The main character is a little less confident than previous ones have been. The supporting cast is a little more active. And the action level is a little more understated than in past books, balanced out by a little more investigation stuff, and a few more irons in the fire.

I like that complexity, a lot. It feels authentic to me for the characters. But I hope I didn't go too far from what those reading the stories are looking for. I guess if you're reading this now, you thought it was okay, so thanks for sticking with it! I promise, future books will have Cait developing her skills and Aza being increasingly awesome (and aggro, of course. He is a dragon, after all).

April is always like the end of a marathon for me. Wrapping up the school year, plus a professional conference I always attend, in non-pandemic times anyway, and planning out my summer work priorities all come together to make the month a blur. It's an interesting blend, personally, of hope, regret, and exhaustion. But I'm excited to dig into the next book of this series, and that has me re-energized. Now, if it would just act like spring and quit snowing in Pittsburgh, that would be great.

I owe a couple of acknowledgements in this one for ideas I borrowed because they just felt right. The daggers in the wrist sheaths, while used in all sorts of fantasy tales, came to me from Laurell K. Hamilton's Anita Blake series. I read the most recent book while writing this one (a rare case of reading in a genre very similar to what I'm writing at the moment), and saw the description of how one was over the arm and one was under. I then spent ten minutes walking around the first floor of my house making strange arm motions as I figured out how the draw would work depending on how the sheaths were worn. There's a lot less twisting to do when they're over/under.

The second is the coven's preference for eating meat or

fish only when it comes from undomesticated animals. That is straight out of CJ Cherryh's amazing *Foreigner* series. As is doubtless obvious by now, Cait's coven is very much grounded in nature. This seems like a choice they would make, as well. Cherryh's take on it is somewhat more complex. I highly recommend the series to anyone who enjoys both Science Fiction and Fantasy.

So far, the Universe is giving me positive signs about my trip at the end of the month. I face it with some trepidation. I haven't been in an airport, nor in an enclosed space with as many people as will be on that plane, since December 2019. And then there's the conference itself, which, again, I've not done anything like in quite a while. Feels like a moment of transition.

My brain is all over the place these days. In recent weeks I've read more *Foreigner,* tried Termination Shock (nope), read Rafael (eh. I liked investigator Blake. I'm less excited by paranormal romance Blake. I recognize that's totally just my preference), gave the new Angel-driven Laurell K. Hamilton book a try (meh), and then went back to Daniel Suarez's *Daemon* and *Freedom, Inc.* They're getting a little dated, but still incredible in plot and worldbuilding.

No big-screen action in the last month. I think the next movie for me will be *Dr. Strange 2.* But lots of small screen. Tried *The Chair.* It's not really my jam, but I'm a fan of Sandra Oh. Picked up Star Trek: Discovery again, and am just so impressed at the degree to which they engage with the original series but are not ruled by it. Really enjoying it, and looking forward to *Strange New Worlds* and *Picard* Season 2.

So, *Moon Knight.* I'm a fan of Marvel (and DC for that

matter), and yet that first episode was a tough one to watch. The way they played out his particular life experience (don't want to spoil for those who haven't seen it) was well done, especially the acting. But it didn't grab me the way that I expected it to. Still, I'll be around for the next one.

Book of Boba Fett just mystifies me. Written by Jon Favreau. Directed by Robert Rodriguez. How do those two make such a SLOW episode? Even the fight scenes and the parkour moved like molasses for me. (Again, maybe that's me. I certainly don't claim I could have done better) I'll give episode two a try, and probably watch them all eventually, but dang. It's *Star Wars*. Get some coffee before the next edit session.

As for me, I'm going to take my own advice, get some more coffee, and get to work on the next book. Wishing you all good things until our paths come together once again.

Reminder yet again - If you're not part of the Oriceran Fans Facebook group, **join**! There's a pizza giveaway every month, and Martha and (usually) I and all sort of fun author folks show up via Zoom to chat with our readers. It's a great time, and the community feel to it is truly fantastic. Oriceran Fans. Facebook. Your phone is probably within reach. Do it!

Before I go, once again, if this series is your first taste of my Urban Fantasy, look for "Magic Ops." I promise you'll enjoy it, and you'll get more of Diana, Rath, and company. You might also enjoy my science fiction work. All my writing is filled with action, snark, and villains who think they're heroes. Drop by www.trcameron.com and take a look!

Until next time, Joys upon joys to you and yours – so may it be.

PS: If you'd like to chat with me, here's the place. I check in daily or more: https://www.facebook.com/AuthorTRCameron. Often I put up interesting and/or silly content there, as well. For more info on my books, and to join my reader's group, please visit www.trcameron.com.

AUTHOR NOTES - MARTHA CARR

MAY 13, 2022

My first job in the world was working at the White House on Pennsylvania Avenue. My big sister, Cary had the job before me - she knew Susan Ford (and looked just like her) and Mom made her give the job to me. I had to go through a federal background check and forgot to tell my references. They thought I had run away or something had happened when the FBI showed up at their door unannounced.

On my first day walking into *the House,* I got lost on the grounds and a Secret Service agent came running and checked my ID again. In those days in 1975 people weren't as worried about security and so it was only one guard and he got over it. When I got inside and saw other guards all of them were greeting me with, "Hello Kiddy." Cary had told them my name was Kiddy because - Kiddy Carr.

President Ford was in office - the second half of his term and occasionally we'd see the teenagers run by our spot. Seconds later the Secret Service agents would run by and ask, "Which way did they go?" We'd point them hopefully in the right direction, but we may have misdirected a couple of times. Not the best security system. Betty Ford made a point of occasionally saying hello. Very gracious. We were the only teenagers who worked in the house and had access everywhere. When the family was out of town and not expected back the head Usher would sometimes take us up to the family quarters for a tour. During our long break between the public and private tours we'd go get ice cream in the Navy dining room and nod to Senators having lunch in there. Or we'd wander to the florist inside the house and practice making arrangements.

When Queen Elizabeth and Prince Phillip came to visit, we were asked to "volunteer" in exchange for seeing the official greeting. We were teenagers so, we said yes. We helped make arrangements and set up under the tent in the rose garden. And of course, we wandered up to the blue room and stood behind all of the place cards on the floor for the official reception line. We watched the greeting on the front lawn from the blue room and apparently took too long. When we went to open a door, Prince Phillip was standing on the other side. We closed it a little too fast and ran from room to room till we came out on the other side of the crowd.

It was a magical night. When I went to get in my car, a Marine guard asked if I'd like an escort so I said, sure, why not. He was in full dress uniform and we walked out arm in arm. My old 1968 Ford Galaxy 500 (an enormous aqua blue car and my Dad's first car he ever bought new - air conditioning at last!) was parked on a side street close to the north side of the house that's no longer a street. When we came outside and got close to the car we could see there were Secret Service checking it for bombs even though there was a pass clearly visible in the front window. The guard did his best not to smile and I drove off with as much dignity as I could muster.

Every Saturday when I worked one of us had to walk the cash to the bank to deposit. No internet in those days. An agent would always accompany us. Once someone blew a nice cloud of weed smoke in our faces as we walked by. The agent shrugged - he had to stay with me and the cash and he wasn't local police so what could he do. It was kind of funny.

The last two years I had the job were during the first years of President Carter's term. On one of his first days I was in the small hallway where there was a narrow elevator from the private quarters to the West Wing. Behind me was a narrow, curving staircase.

One bell softly chimed letting us know that the President was coming down and I got out of the way of the doors and silently waited. We had been told more than once to not speak to the President if they passed by. I waited and waited but the doors didn't open and a smile was growing on the face of the agent standing in front of me.

"What?" I asked.

"The President is behind you. He came down the stairs."

I froze. I hadn't even heard him on the stairs. "What do I do?"

The agent laughed and waved. "Step forward."

I walked toward the agent and turned around as President Carter passed us. He rarely did things according to protocol. State dinners during his term were alcohol free and anyone who worked for him couldn't live with a partner unless they were married.

Some of the agents in the house were regularly picking up women tourists in the line coming through the house. The other teenager who worked with me and I would sidle up near the married agents who had a reputation for picking up the women and showing them the bowling alley. We'd ask in a loud voice, "How's the wife? She had that baby yet" to shoo away the women.

One agent came over to the North Portico where we stood to sell the books and asked me out one day when I was knew. When I explained I was fifteen the color drained from his face and he scooted away and never came back to that side of the house.

It was an amazing job. I saw celebrities (Jamie Farr, the Beach Boys - and got backstage passes to their concert) and a cross section of America and humanity in general and got to wander through the Map Room and the East Wing at will and by myself any time I wanted and admire Monets and the portraits and take a spin in the East ballroom. Perfect job for a dreamy teenager who wanted to grow up and be a writer. More adventures to follow.

OTHER SERIES IN THE ORICERAN UNIVERSE:

THE LEIRA CHRONICLES
CASE FILES OF AN URBAN WITCH
THE EVERMORES CHRONICLES
SOUL STONE MAGE
THE KACY CHRONICLES
MIDWEST MAGIC CHRONICLES
THE FAIRHAVEN CHRONICLES
I FEAR NO EVIL
THE DANIEL CODEX SERIES
SCHOOL OF NECESSARY MAGIC
SCHOOL OF NECESSARY MAGIC: RAINE CAMPBELL
ALISON BROWNSTONE
FEDERAL AGENTS OF MAGIC
SCIONS OF MAGIC
THE UNBELIEVABLE MR. BROWNSTONE
DWARF BOUNTY HUNTER
ACADEMY OF NECESSARY MAGIC
MAGIC CITY CHRONICLES
ROGUE AGENTS OF MAGIC

OTHER SERIES IN THE ORICERAN UNIVERSE:

OTHER BOOKS BY JUDITH BERENS

OTHER BOOKS BY MARTHA CARR

JOIN THE ORICERAN UNIVERSE FAN GROUP ON FACEBOOK!

CONNECT WITH THE AUTHORS

TR Cameron Social

Website: www.trcameron.com

Facebook: https://www.facebook.com/AuthorTRCameron

Martha Carr Social

Website: http://www.marthacarr.com

Facebook: https://www.facebook.com/groups/MarthaCarrFans/

Michael Anderle Social

Website: http://lmbpn.com

Email List: http://lmbpn.com/email/

https://www.facebook.com/LMBPNPublishing

https://twitter.com/MichaelAnderle

https://www.instagram.com/lmbpn_publishing/

https://www.bookbub.com/authors/michael-anderle

BOOKS BY MICHAEL ANDERLE

Sign up for the LMBPN email list to be notified of new releases and special deals!

https://lmbpn.com/email/

For a complete list of books by Michael Anderle, please visit:

www.lmbpn.com/ma-books/

Printed in Great Britain
by Amazon